PURSUITS OF MOXXI

PURSUITS OF MOXXI

Z. Ham

&

A. P. Goodman

ISBN 978-1-964980-02-7 (pb)

Book Cover by Nitish Mathpal

Visit us on the Web!
www.apgoodman.com

First edition 2025

To Z. Ham,

Thank you for breathing life into this story and making it your own. You are talented beyond your years, and watching your mind create and mold these characters from scratch has been nothing short of amazing. I am always in awe of you and your beautiful brain. Never change. You are a diamond in the rough, and I can't wait for the world to get a glimpse of how bright you shine.

Table of Contents

1. Part I
2. Part II
3. Part III
4. Part IV
5. Part V
6. Part VI
7. Part VII
8. Part VIII
9. Part IX
10. Part X

E. Epilogue

Part I

Ninety-two. That's how many afterworlds Moxxi had traveled to in the past nine days. It was the most souls they had ever delivered in that amount of time, and they never wanted their duties to be that rigorous again. The mess they had walked into at Legacy Academy was astronomical. The school was filled with displaced souls, unaffectionately called The Nulls. Worlds had been destroyed, and the few entities that were saved wound up at the school. However, being rescued from their imploding worlds was the extent of the care offered. The Nulls had received food and shelter but not much else. The mass of beings were forgotten as quickly as they were rescued until Moxxi arrived.

Moxxi knew almost immediately that they should've called for help of some kind: a backup transporter, an assistant, something. Anyone who could reap a soul would have been sufficient enough, but ego had gotten the best of them. They had never asked for help before and certainly had no intention to on their first mission outside of Prague. In the end, they did what they always did: They got the job done. All one hundred and forty-seven souls had been dispatched to the assigned afterlives by Moxxi, and now, the transporter was exhausted beyond belief.

Moxxi thought for sure that the first task, once their overwhelming burdens were finished, was going to be enjoying unlimited relaxation. They had frequently fantasized about turning into a shadow and curling up in a dark corner somewhere. Their underground dungeon in Prague sounded ideal, especially if there was a way to eliminate all the noisy tourists that came by. How Moxxi wished to solve that problem themself, but using their powers for anything other than their designated responsibilities would land them in serious trouble with their patron, Mors, and an encounter with the Roman God of Death was not something to be taken lightly. They hadn't seen him in the past half century, and that was the way they preferred it. That said, daydreaming of a small fire blocking the entrance to their favorite corridor replayed frequently in their mind.

However, when the time came, and the final soul had been dropped off to Tech Duinn, going back to Prague felt uninspiring. They were far more restless than anticipated. This feeling was new to Moxxi. Not wanting to resume their post wasn't like them. Staying in one place had always been Moxxi's preference. If they remained stationary, they could ensure their territory was properly cared for. If their territory was properly cared for, the souls of that region would be cared for as well, and Moxxi's obligations would be fulfilled.

They felt confident in their ability to cover one area thoroughly and efficiently. That's what they did, and had done, for . . . well . . . for their entire existence. It didn't make sense to spread themself thin and do partial jobs all over the world. Transporting the dead to their proper resting place was already enough travel. They didn't exist to see the world. They were here to rescue the helpless. Prague supplied them with a vast array of souls to deal with. That particular niche of the Czech Republic rarely had a lull in unclaimed spirits. It kept them busy, productive even. Moxxi had always equated their worth with their productivity, but today, they craved for a change in routine. The fresh air felt kind of nice.

They debated where to go. Conflicting emotions whirled inside of them. They could've stayed in Ireland. They could've tried out Olympus. There were a lot of places they could have gone, maybe even should have gone, but while they fought their internal battle, they found themselves high on a mountain staring down at the town of Astoria. After everything, they found themselves focused, once again, on Legacy Academy. They suspected they could've gone there too. They were sure Shadow Boy and Bright Eyes would have welcomed them gladly. However, being in that school gave off the same vibe their favorite dungeon was giving them: imprisonment.

They were tired of being restrained by their own made-up rules. They wanted to be free. They wanted to live in a way they had never felt before. They wanted a life outside of just being a transporter. They wanted to learn what it meant to be Moxxi. With a deep breath, they knew what they had to do: It was time to break free of old chains and chart their own course.

They scaled down the mountain range with ease and never let themself rest. They marveled at the coldness of the snow on the cliffs, the tightened pathways of the forests, the wetness of the various lakes and rivers. They admired the stillness of the plains and rolled down more than one hill simply because they could. They felt the Earth, the one place all the souls of every belief system had in common. They basked in every ray of sunshine and let themself be soaked by every raindrop within their reach. They never sought out shelter from a storm. They withstood it all and refused to stop walking until their god-like body spurned their pursuit.

Once their body left them with no other choice, they turned into their shadow form under a cold, dark, star-filled sky and found solace under a rocky archway. The structure looked almost like a portal into another world. Their landing spot did not disappoint.

Even though the land was dark, its voice was loud. Cries from the past echoed along the quartzite hallways and tunnels below. This area was dense and rich in culture. Voices here demanded retribution.

There would be unlimited opportunities and encounters to unpack here if they chose to accept them. Moxxi could feel the excitement within them rise as names of unfamiliar deities were shouted around them. There was almost an absolute guarantee that new gateways to the otherworlds took residence in this area. Moxxi decided they were ready for it. They were ready to explore. They were ready to see new things, but it all had to wait until morning.

~*~

Slipping into the dreamworld proved to be tumultuous. Nightmares ran rampant in this canyon. The chaos was both consuming and overwhelming. There was a current to the discord. It would pull you in, almost lure you in, and then crush you with its agonizing intensity, only to repeat the cycle again and again. It made its prey want to run deeper into the web of madness to avoid the pain that it created behind them, a pain that never seemed to stop closing in on their current location.

Moxxi had never encountered a vortex like this before. They immediately knew it was unnatural. Even the most distraught mass of humans would be unable to form a maelstrom like this. The sea of dreams was a fragile place. It was easily influenced and easily manipulated, but all within certain boundaries. Whatever this whirlpool was, was defying the basic parameters set by Morpheus, and Moxxi could only imagine the dangers that surrounded a situation like that. Defying the laws of a god never ended well.

How could things have gotten this bad? Is another entity forcing this upon the world? If something in the world is so obviously opposing the work of Morpheus, why hasn't he stepped in and stopped it? Moxxi gave pause to think. There was only one answer that ever made a god give up control of their domain, and that was something much, much worse.

If a deity opposing Morpheus was further up the pantheon pyramid, or even equal to Morpheus' level, Moxxi was certain the intruder would have been dealt with already. Greco-Roman gods reveled in handling their own family drama. It may very well be the one thing they loved more than their own ego.

Who is higher up than Morpheus? Hypnos? Somnus? Another mythological equivalent? Moxxi had never dealt with inter-mythology hierarchies. They weren't sure how any of that meshed together. They gave a brief thought to where Mors would be in respect to Morpheus, in case that came into play later, but the nagging feeling that this could be the work of another belief system entirely overtook their mind.

There were so many names filling their ears that they didn't recognize as they drifted off to sleep. The souls, the land, everything here vibrated at a completely different frequency than what they were used to. Moxxi knew they didn't know enough to find the answers they wanted and promised themself they'd find out more tomorrow.

Moxxi hadn't realized that traveling to these lands would be so unexpected. It hadn't occurred to them that new territories meant new people. And that new people meant new belief systems, and new belief systems meant entirely new divine families and pantheons. After having just traveled to almost one hundred different afterworlds, Moxxi never fathomed being confronted by something unknown. New never happened in Prague. Prague was older than old and, while it was probably the most haunted town in the world, it was as predictable as ever.

Part of Moxxi wanted to run to Mors. He had to have more he could teach them, but part of them also wanted a challenge. They wanted to prove how strong they were to themself. Their life had been a standard routine for decades, and now, they were on the edge of something completely unexpected.

Maybe new is good? Moxxi got closer to the nearest nightmare in this dreamworld. *Maybe . . . I like new?*

Without much forethought, they touched the vision before them, like a moth drawing closer to a flame. The orb's reaction was immediate. They were instantly catapulted into the swirly mix their eyes had fixated on. Shrieks of lost souls filled their ears; tear-stained faces desperately leapt to hold onto Moxxi as they ripped through the world these former humans were trapped in. The weight of heartbreak and despair knew no bounds in this dream. People of all ages, all races, were mixed together, bound by their hopelessness.

Ten. Twenty. Fifty? One hundred and fifty?

Moxxi did their best to estimate the number of beings they flew past. They had just begun to lose count when they landed in a dimly lit room, thrusted sternly into a hard, unforgiving wall. They were disoriented. Their mind had been overloaded. The only thing they could process was the quiet intermittent beep of a machine as it replaced the whirlpool of screams.

~*~

Moxxi couldn't tell how long it had taken for them to physically get back up onto their own two feet again. Their head was fuzzy and buzzed with ferocity. Their feet were unsteady, and they stumbled even when they weren't trying to move at all. Their energy was drained. They felt depleted of life. The fact that they were still in their solid form was more of a surprise than not. They didn't know what part of them was able to sustain this form. They barely had the energy to keep their eyes open.

As they tried to adjust to the wavering light, they swore they saw a young child walk in front of the door. The girl was small, she could not be more than five or six, and she held a dangly, raggedy, brown rabbit in her arms. Her walk was slow, steady, and felt deliberate.

Moxxi tried to move towards her, but their legs weren't strong enough. They stumbled into a cart, a medical cart. The noise disturbance caught the attention of the little girl. She turned to face Moxxi. Her petite frame instantly took on a defensive stance. Her face was doused with fear.

For the first time, Moxxi surveyed their surroundings. They were in a large hospital room. An empty bed was behind them. Needing the extra support, they let themself fall upon it as they greeted the child. Moxxi tried to lift an arm to wave. Their movements were jerky and awkward.

The girl bolted at the sight.

Moxxi felt deflated. They were just trying to help.

They went to call out to the child, to let her know she was safe, but a darkness was starting to creep into the space. Moxxi couldn't tell if their vision was failing or if it was something more. It didn't look like a shadow. Shadows were familiar and fluid. This void was dense and clouded their entire peripheral vision.

Moxxi used the cart they had slipped on earlier as a crutch and scooted towards the doorway. They pursued the path the child had run in, but she was nowhere to be found. The hall was completely unoccupied except for an expansive mass of gloom at its end. Cursing to themself, they understood the responsibility forced upon them.

"Here we go again." Moxxi whispered aloud as they propelled themselves and their cart directly into the center of the pulsating blackness.

~*~

Double doors opened beside Moxxi as they went through the passageway into the new area. The air felt lighter here, almost weightless. Moxxi had been braced for intensity, but much to their surprise, the void seemed to be filled with emptiness. The space they walked into was unoccupied and eerily quiet. There was nothing here; no one was around. The absence of life felt haunting.

A yellowish light blinked ahead. As the single bulb flickered, others came to life as well. Numerous flat-panel lights began to illuminate the ceiling. They created an endless sea of yellow. The lights, the ceiling, the walls, even the flooring was now tinged with a hint of off-white yellow. Moxxi thought it to be an interesting color, not quite yellow, not quite white. It reminded Moxxi of the color of creamed corn. *Why would someone douce their space with the color of creamed corn?*

Moxxi carefully took a step forward, very aware that the aid they were using for support was nowhere to be seen. It didn't hurt. In fact, as Moxxi subtly checked their range of motion throughout their body, no part of them hurt. They were not unaware of where their pain should be, but it was like there was a thick barrier between what they knew existed and what they actually felt. For all intents and purposes, they were currently pain-free.

Skeptical, Moxxi studied their location. They walked down the vacant center aisle. Half-walls framed the walkway with wide berths in between them. Periodic columns, small in width, ornamented the open side-spaces. They were more structural than functional. Nothing offered concealment here. Moxxi supposed they should find solace in that; there was no place for surprises to hide here. However, as they progressed deeper and deeper into the almond-yellow room, their conscience kept reminding them of one thing: *There's nowhere for me to hide here either.*

They picked up their pace, trying to find a safety net among the yellow-tinged scenery. Nothing. More manilla walls, more manilla pillars, more open space. The repetition was almost dizzying, and the constant smell of musty dampness was messing with Moxxi's stomach. They continued their fast-paced walk. Only the center aisle remained as a viable walkway. It never turned. It just went straight on forever. Moxxi couldn't say for certain, but at one point they felt the room looped a repeated pattern. They dug into their pockets for some type of object to mark their surroundings and test their theory. Eventually, they found a rock stuck to the bottom of their shoe. They scraped a deep X onto the closest surface. Now, they'd know for certain if they were going in circles.

A rumbling came from an unknown location. The floor below Moxxi's feet started to shake. The air was beginning to hold a strange vibration. *That noise wasn't human.* Sweat began to form on the back of Moxxi's neck. Whatever was coming wasn't from the normal world. Flashes of underworld beasts flipped rapidly in their mind, beasts of nightmares and the darkest tales of mythology, beasts no one should ever have to encounter face-to-face, yet seemed to be the norm in Moxxi's duties.

Moxxi debated the best strategy. If they went towards the noise, they would find out what the threat was sooner. Perhaps, they would be familiar with the creature and know how to handle it. But . . . if they didn't . . . time was of the essence.

Moxxi broke out into a fast jog and attempted to use their momentum as an energy source to change into their shadow-like form, but their efforts were fruitless. They screamed at themself, "Work!"

A distorted ear-piercing growl roared back.

They were confident now that no matter what was in this place, it wasn't anything Moxxi had previous knowledge of. They shook their hand to materialize their torch. An image flickered, almost tangible. "Come on!! You've never failed me before. Don't start now!" The room was shaking strongly; Moxxi's vision blurred before them. They closed their eyes and trusted their instincts. The torch refused to fully form in their hand. They followed their gut.

"I can do this. I can do this." They reiterated continuously. *Straight. Left. Left. Right.*

The smell was dissipating. The scent of wet carpet was being replaced by . . . fresh fish? "What?" Moxxi opened their eyes. The manilla environment had not let go of its formation, but the room was rotated ninety degrees. Everything looked the way it always had, but somehow, Moxxi knew they were no longer oriented in the same direction. They wished they had a compass to verify what they felt.

A high-pitched shriek erupted from behind them.

Moxxi turned to face their adversary when a small hand reached out from a nearby wall beside them and yanked them through.

Part II

"You're welcome."

"I'm sorry?" Moxxi righted themself and got up off the dirty cement.

"I said you're welcome." A small boy walked in the opposite direction of the wall he had just pulled Moxxi through.

Moxxi didn't want to chase after him, but it was clear that he was not sticking around to chat. "I didn't say thank you."

"You should have." He noticed Moxxi making strange movements of their body. He tensed, ready for this new person to be yet another trick of the realm, but when Moxxi started to grunt in frustration, relief filled his body. "You're not very good at this, are you?"

"You're quite rude for a child," Moxxi stated condescendingly. They tried to shift into their shadow form again. *Why does this keep failing? This never fails.*

"I don't know what you're trying to do, but assuming you're actually trying to do something and not completely losing your mind, I would save your energy. This place will take anything it can from you before you even notice that it's gone."

Moxxi scoffed. "That's optimistic."

"Optimism gets you killed. Ask my sister."

That was enough to stop Moxxi's steps. Moxxi hadn't thought to look for other souls here. They certainly hadn't felt any, but the image of the little girl with the bunny was still at the front of their mind. Staring at the boy from behind, Moxxi noticed how similar his hair was to the little girl's, how similar his walk was to hers. "She carried a brown stuffed rabbit with her, didn't she?"

He spun on his heels. "You saw Brownie?" His eyes went wide with a flood of emotions.

"Is that her name? Brownie?" Moxxi thought that was a funny name for a child but wasn't going to judge.

"What? No. That's her stuffie. Who would name a child Brownie?"

Moxxi knew better than to respond. Arguing with small humans was not worth their time.

"Was she back in the lobby? We have to go back!" He took off running back towards the wall they had just left.

Moxxi caught him in their arms. "No. I saw her in a hospital. I got pulled there from a dream and then saw her walk into a dark void. She's how I ended up here." *Maybe she did want me to follow her in here after all?*

Feeling instant defeat, the boy's body slumped in response. "I guess you better meet the others then." He pushed away from Moxxi. "Follow me."

Skeptically, Moxxi accompanied the churlish boy and sized up the new area. Where the past area had been repetitive, manilla, and damp-smelling, this new area was raw, moist, and foggy. Though, to no surprise, the fog was slightly tinged the creamed corn color of the previous lair. Whatever god ruled over this domain had a serious obsession with the color yellow. The floor here was composed of old, dirty, chipped concrete with paint marks that reminded Moxxi of parking spaces. Random pillars still appeared in the walkways, but they were made of metal beams and raw unprotected wiring. The light was blinking here, as it did before, but there was a higher contrast. The illuminated spots were brighter, and the shadows were darker. Moxxi looked to the ceiling, anticipating the buzz and glow of never-ending fluorescent lighting, and found them without coverings. The bulbs were bright, thin, and exposed, barely stable in their swaying fixtures.

"Where are we?" Moxxi meant to say to themself but accidently spoke it aloud.

"We're not totally sure. Harps got us to call it The Backrooms." He explained flatly.

"The Backrooms? Because we're in the back of the hospital? If this is the parking lot . . . wouldn't that be The Underrooms?"

The boy stopped, turned to face Moxxi, and with the most annoyed and indignant face his small self could muster, he firmly spat out the word, "No."

Moxxi put their hands up in defense. *Note to self: Don't try to clarify the lore that's already been decided, unintelligent or not.*

The boy sighed harshly. "We're almost there. When you meet everyone, be cool. Okay? I don't want them thinking I brought some lame noob into the group."

"Lame noob? What does that even mean?"

"It means don't suck." He rolled his eyes at his new guest and continued on towards an angled wall. He reached into the corner of the wall and pulled back a sheet, not keeping it open behind him.

He was trying Moxxi's patience. They reached for the same corner and noticed their hand was completely covered in a shadow. They tried once more to turn into shadow form. Other than a strong jerk of the curtain, nothing happened.

"What are you doing? Are you trying to ruin our cover? Get in here, you noob!" The boy yanked on Moxxi's clothing and pulled them in.

"Azi! What—" An exasperated face appeared in the dim light. "—who?" They changed their focus to meet Moxxi's eyes. They were tall and presumably much closer to Moxxi's chosen age than the child that led them here was. Their skin was light and thin, almost giving off a translucent appearance, which provided a stark contrast to their wildly chopped jet-black hair. "Why are you here? He shouldn't have brought you."

Nice to meet you too. I am also pleased to meet your acquaintance, Moxxi mocked internally. "Hello, I'm Moxxi."

"I don't care. I asked why you're here."

"Because he brought me." Moxxi delivered with a shrug.

"You don't belong here. You need to leave."

With pleasure. If I only knew how.

"Harps." The boy tugged at the bottom of her torn shirt, trying to stay out of view and side-eyeing Moxxi. "Harper!" He whisper-yelled.

"Azi. You can't just bring people here. They need to leave. Having more people with us isn't safe." There was almost a hint of compassion to her voice.

"Harps!" His whispered yells were increasing in volume. "They saw Brownie." His delivery was emotional. Moxxi could see a glint in his eyes even with the poor lighting. "I couldn't let them walk away if they knew something about Amari."

Harper's shoulders sank, and she put her arm around the boy she called Azi and kissed his head. "We'll find her. I promise."

Moxxi looked away. Whatever this moment was between those two seemed incredibly private. Their extra presence felt intrusive even to themself.

"Hey. Blondie. What's your name?"

These people couldn't be more charming if they tried. Moxxi met Harper's inquisition with a soft smile. “Hello. I introduced myself earlier. My name is Moxxi.”

“Moxxi.” Harper let the new name hang in the air like they were waiting to see if it passed some invisible test. “All right. Moxxi it is then.” She offered a sincere handshake.

Unsure what else to do, Moxxi obliged.

“Welcome to The Backrooms. Hopefully, it won’t last long.” Harper dropped Moxxi’s hand, gave an affirming nod, and retreated to the refuge beyond the entryway.

“We don’t have much, but if you need food, or drink, we have some to share. Just don’t take more than your allotment. It’s rude.” Azi stated with conviction. “Even if they have your FAVORITE treat, and your sister is missing, and you’re REAL sad, you still can’t take it from someone else. Even if you’re friends . . .” He paused and then almost cut himself off, “No! Wait! ESPECIALLY if they’re friends.” He seemed satisfied this time. “Friends don’t steal from friends.”

Moxxi was going to need time to get used to his monologuing. They were grateful when he looked as if he was going to follow Harper into the back.

He grabbed a funny looking gadget and turned on a light from it. “You can leave your stuff here if you have any stuff. Do you got stuff?” He started snooping around Moxxi’s body.

Moxxi did not like that at all. “No stuff. Only personal space.”

He huffed. “We don’t got stuff either. One day

though, one day we'll have stuff."

"That's why it's so great that Amari still has her bunny. She'd never do okay without that lame rabbit."

From an unseen spot, Harper called out. "We all have something, Azi. It's important to not lose focus of what we've been able to hold on to, even if it's small."

"Nu-uh! What stuff you got, Harps? You don't have any stuff."

"I have my bracelet." A slight jingle could be heard not too far away.

"Naw. That's a medical bracelet! That doesn't count. Stuff is like a cool toy or pretty jewelry, not something that says you got the diabetes."

Diabetes. I've transported souls that have had that.

"It's special because it's mine, Azi. It means something to me."

The boy rolled his eyes and let out an annoyed noise. "Yeah, yeah. You go on with your disease bracelet. I want something more than that."

Moxxi found a crate that seemed sturdy enough to sit upon. "If you could have anything, what would you pick?" It felt like a valid enough question. Moxxi had only been here a short amount of time and was already feeling the loss of their skills. They wondered how long Azi and Harper had been suffering their losses.

"Anything? You mean it?" His eyes were round

with wonder.

"I can't give it to you." Moxxi felt it necessary to clarify their question. "But, yeah. If you could have any of your previous possessions, what would you pick?"

"And it doesn't have to be Amari?" He double checked. "Because I would pick my sister before I'd pick any of my toys!" he said firm and proud before sheepishly countering with, "But I wouldn't mind having my toys again, too."

"Of course Armari is first, but this would be a thing just for you. Something you could carry with you," Moxxi assured.

"I used to have this big red fish I really liked. It had red gummy fish inside. They were my favorite. I liked that it had treats, but I could also smack people with it. I couldn't smack Amari with it though. I did that once, and she cried forever, and mom got SO MAD at me she took my fish away. She promised not to tell my dad because he would not take that well at all, and I was happy that he wouldn't know, but I REALLY wanted my fish back, and I was REALLY worried I would never get it back."

Moxxi was amused. "That sounds like a fun toy. Did you ever get it back?"

"I found it! And I took it back. And Mom saw, but she only gave me a look. And not like a 'You've done it, now you're in so much trouble' look either, it was like a 'I see what you've done there, but I'll let you slide this time' look. Those are the best looks. I don't like the 'you're in trouble' looks. Do you ever get those looks?" There was a deep interest behind his question.

His sincerity reminded Moxxi of being back in Astoria. "I do not. Do you?"

He inclined his head to the back where Harper retreated to earlier. "Harps does sometimes, and Gwen too, but a lot less. Oh. Hey." His eyes were scanning the area for something. "Harper! Where's Gwen?"

"She's on patrol."

"Alone? Why would you let her go out there alone? That sounds like a horrible idea!"

"Is Gwen going out there alone a worse decision than a five-year-old going out there alone without telling anyone first?"

Moxxi bit back their lips. This reminded them of the tales they had heard about family squabbles. They had always wondered what that was like.

"I had my reasons!"

"And Gwen has hers."

"Gwen isn't responsible for saving her lost sister!"

"You're right. She wasn't worried about her SISTER." Irritation rising, Harper made sure to emphasize her last word.

Azi went to reply but something got caught in his throat.

Oh . . . Gwen went out looking for him.

Azi started to speak and stopped himself several times before he finally found the right words. "Did you set up the wind-up thingy?"

Harper was quiet in her reply. "I did."

Tears were evident in Azi's voice. He clearly understood a concept Moxxi did not. "Did it stop?"

"Yes." Harper's voice was a whisper.

"How long ago?"

"It's playing its second go through."

"You waited TWO TURNS?! How could you do that to her?!" Azi was in full hysterics.

Moxxi had no idea what was transpiring before them.

"One: Keep your voice down, unless you would like a Disguiser to find us before we even start to find Gwen. Two: You weren't back by the time the first round finished. I couldn't leave without you." Harper's words were intermittent. "I can't lo—" She took a shaky breath. "I can't lose you both."

"She's not lost and neither am I. We have to go out NOW. It'll be too late otherwise. What's the click count?"

The sounds of Harper blowing her nose and wiping it with her sleeve filled the space before she stepped into view. She was holding a wooden object triangular in shape. It had a metal piece in front that wiggled as she walked. She set it atop a crate. "330. Two full rounds."

Azi shook his head. "Was she going up or down?"

"Up." Harper was putting on a jacket and filling

a backpack as she spoke.

"Did you pack her almond water?"

"Yeah. I'm ready. You?"

Azi stood up tall and patted his chest. "I'm ready."

Harper addressed Moxxi. "I hope you aren't scared of dogs."

"Dogs?" Moxxi asked, their voice sounding raspier than intended.

Azi reached for Harper's hand and called out her name hesitantly.

"Dogs." Harper stated flatly to her small counterpart. She waited until he nodded in agreement. "Let's go."

Part III

Moxxi followed along blindly, unsure of what to say or do. Every action seemed more confusing than the last. Harper had led the trio out of the hideout and up a staircase that oddly blended into the wall alongside it. At the top was an elevator. Moxxi had received strict warnings not to make a single sound inside. Harper had even emphasized they try to hold their breath in if possible. They doubted that was necessary but did so out of caution anyway.

The trek was almost incident free, until off in the distance, an extra-large spider, at least a foot in width, made Moxxi gasp with fright. When Harper turned to glare at them, they pantomimed the description of the crawling insect. Harper was not fazed and squinted with scrutiny at them, but Moxxi's face held in a grimace, and their eyes were frozen round as they forced Harper to acknowledge the creature of concern.

Harper's face flushed at the moving silhouette. She immediately forced the group to sprint through the narrow hallways filled with copper pipes. Moxxi's sides ached with pain, and even Azi started to groan with complaints. Harper remained steadfast until breathlessly, arriving at a boiler room and ensuring the door had been secured behind all three of them.

Moxxi's hands clutched their stomach. "I. Don't. Run." They wished more than ever that they could return to their shadow form to traverse this realm. Their physical body was not used to being pushed to limits like this. They had felt drained back in the hospital, and that seemed like a lifetime ago with no rest in between.

"I suggest you start," Harper advised.

Moxxi expected more condescension in her tone.

"I'm not falling behind and finding out what comes next if you can't keep up," Harper spat bluntly.

Azi stirred in discomfort. "But Harps . . . Brownie."

"I'm sorry, Azi, but your new friend needs to keep up. I can't have them slacking and risk myself, you, or Gwen when we finally get her back."

Moxxi had met souls like Harper in their previous duties. Souls that were vigilant, dutiful, and militant. There were not a lot of spirits belonging to great war veterans in Prague, but there had been some to trickle in over the years. The last one that Moxxi had to help transport was handed off to a Valkyrie. It was the first time they had seen that particular type of warrior goddess. Their cheeks reddened. What they wouldn't give to have one of the Norse angels here right now. The Valkyries were the epitome of beauty and brawn. There was nothing they couldn't do. Moxxi had never met a being so immaculate before. They were the eternal battle maiden.

Thoughts of living a life in battle hit differently now that Moxxi was trapped in The Backrooms. If Prague was a prison cell, The Backrooms was an entire warzone. "How long have you been living like this?" Moxxi pushed out the words despite the muscles in their torso spasming.

Harper blew off the question. She had no time for unimportant nonsense. "I don't know? A while?"

That answer was vaguer than a Greek prophecy. Moxxi tried to hide their eye roll.

"Are you two done sitting yet?" The lack of patience was prudent in Harper's question.

"Yeah. Yeah. I'm good. I could've kept going. I just thought we should stop for Moxxi's sake. They looked like they were struggling." Azi coughed as he replied.

Harper's look softened. "I know."

Moxxi did not believe a word of it, but they were not about to start an argument with a five-year-old. "What's next?"

"The darkness." Harper made eye contact sizing up Moxxi's reaction.

Finally, something that sounds familiar. Moxxi smiled. "I think I can handle that."

Harper's stare never broke focus. "We'll see.

Won't we?"

Azi broke the tension. Moxxi watched as he slid his hand into Harper's and laid his head on her shoulder, neither mentioning anything.

Harper rested her head on his before dictating their next steps. "I have a flashlight if we need it, but that'll only bring attention to us. Stay quiet, stay low, and keep out of the light. And whatever you do, do not go towards any music."

Moxxi laughed at the juxtaposition of this desolate world and the silliness of a catchy tune. "Gotcha. No time for a dance party."

Azi wasn't taking the situation lightly. "No, Moxxi. Seriously. No music, got it? You can't go. No food either. This is the most important!" His chest was rising and falling rapidly.

"Hey, hey. It's okay. It was a bad joke. You lead, I follow. I got it." Guilt flooded over Moxxi and only intensified when they saw Harper's pursed-lip expression.

Her tone was borderline threatening when she addressed the situation. "Don't screw this up for us."

Moxxi wanted to offer their sincerest guarantee. They wanted to promise both Harper and Azi that not only were they not totally useless, they actually were quite special, remarkable even, but there was no path that made sense for that conversation, especially with their current inability to harness any of the skills they relied so desperately upon.

Moxxi had been to multiple worlds curated for

a mortal's afterlife. They had navigated through hellish pits, eruptions of lava, and ensnaring traps. They had been chased by demigods, demons, and devils. They had saved hundreds of souls trapped between worlds, and none of it seemed to matter. Moxxi knew they were exceptional and powerful, but it felt so past tense. All they could do at this moment was make a mediocre promise that they were not even sure they would keep. "I won't."

"Go where I go." Azi comforted. He slipped his free hand into Moxxi's.

Why is he holding my hand? No one had ever done that before. It felt . . . safe. It was strange. Too new, too unexpected. Caught up in the surprise of his action, Moxxi didn't think to resist when he pulled them onwards. They didn't even notice when they had been guided into a dismal abyss. By the time their brain caught up, they couldn't tell the difference between their eyes being open or closed.

The tricky thing about a pitch-black room is that your mind starts to compensate for the lack of visual activity. At first, Moxxi's mind only tried to trick them with periodic spots. Ones where the color isn't actually a color, but it resembles a yellow-purple-metallic mix match. Sometimes one large blotch would appear, sometimes three or four smaller blotches clustered together. Some would linger and some could be seen in short bursts. Sometimes they were barely even circular and looked more like a smear, that almost resembled a contorted mouth. No matter what the combination, the distortions always lingered in the corner of Moxxi's peripheral vision.

The deeper Moxxi went, the more creative liberties their mind was willing to take on. They felt the room begin to spin. They clutched onto Azi's hand as they were sure they were walking sideways at one point. He shook them off but grabbed hold of them again quickly. They found themself relieved that he came back so quickly. Moxxi was sure if he had actually let go, they would be lost forever in this upside-down darkness.

This way and that, Moxxi walked in dizzying circles, absolutely sure that their feet were on the sides of walls and defying gravity from one end to the other. Moxxi had never been one to feel motion sickness before, but the sensation was rising within them and closing in on its peak. Just as Moxxi was formulating the best way to throw up, the trio stopped.

Silence was thick and heavy around them. Not a sound was heard and not a movement was made. It was clear that they were waiting for something, but Moxxi had no idea what. They thought to sit down, their feet were already hurting before this journey began, but Azi hadn't moved an inch, so they decided it was best if they didn't either.

The noise came on faintly, like a melody softly playing in the swirl of a breeze. It was dainty and delicate. It twirled around them, and Moxxi wanted so badly to sway along with the notes. It was calming and pleasant. Everything this place was not.

Ignore the music Moxxi, they warned you about this. Moxxi reminded themself. *But how could a tune this light and airy be considered a bad thing?*

Moxxi had seen plenty of horrible things in their life. Anger, hostility, rage, spite, all of those things were commonplace in Moxxi's life. But this . . . this was gentle and carefree. *Isn't this what we want for ourselves? Isn't this what most mortals are dying to obtain?* Their head and neck were the first to disobey the statuesque rigidness that was being imposed on their body. Swaying left to right, Moxxi felt as if they were conducting their own masterful piece of music. The song hit every note perfectly, and each was more harmonious than the last. Their shoulders and upper arms fell victim to the rhythm next. Stress and worry were leaving Moxxi's body, and peace almost felt like a tangible reality. Moxxi had never known true inner peace, and the thought was more delightful than Moxxi could have put into words. They understood why so many souls asked about it.

A bright burning light seared Moxxi's vision. They felt fingers holding their eyelids open. Moxxi fought back, trying to blink, trying to squirm out of their reach.

"They're coming back!" Azi cheered gleefully.

"Fantastic, if they could come back before Happy Face does, that would be incredibly helpful."

Moxxi pushed their eyes closed and shook their head forcefully, breaking away from their detainment. “What in the heavens are you two doing?” Moxxi shouted, recoiling from their touch.

“Saving you!” Harper criticized. “You didn’t ignore the music, did you?”

Azi whispered angrily from behind them, “I TOLD you, Moxxi. NO music.”

“It was exquisite. Which is more than I can say for whatever you two were doing to me! What was that?”

“A flashlight.” Harper shone the beam straight into Moxxi’s face again, eyeing them skeptically.

“What is your problem? Why did you do that? Where are we?” Moxxi’s agitation was growing by the second. Thoughts of splitting up and striking out on their own were surging within them. They felt distrust and resentment boiling to the surface.

“Listen, I know that wasn’t pleasant, all right? But I didn’t have a choice. You gave in really quickly. You didn’t even try to fight the enchantment. So, we did what we had to do. To save you, remember that part? The part where we didn’t let you get eaten or whatever it is that Happy Face does. I don’t want to think about it. But now, you’re conscious, and we need to go.”

“I highly doubt anything you would do was in my best interest, Harper Quake.” A moment of confusion flushed over Moxxi. “If that even is your real name . . .” They added uncertainly. *Had she ever told me her last name? Why did I say that?*

“Yeah. I’m done. I’m sorry, Azi.” Harper went to

flip off the flashlight when Azi's hands stopped her.

"Harps."

"We can't waste any more time here, or with them. We need to go find Gwen."

The notes of a music box began to play a new song. They recognized this one. Moxxi searched to find the source of the tune while humming along. *All around the mulberry bush, the monkey chased the weasel; the monkey thought twas all in fun, pop goes the weasel . . .*

"Crap!" Harper grabbed Azi's arm hard. "RUN!"

With seconds to think, he grabbed and pulled Moxxi along too. He was literally dragging Moxxi with him by the collar of their shirt when they found who, or rather what, they had been looking for.

The flashlight bounced beams of light off the room as Harper ran, giving Moxxi glimpses of the horror they were fleeing from. The entity's eyes were like a spider. Four glowing symmetric orbs hovering near each other. Their body was amorphous. The shape changed every time Moxxi blinked at the figure. Blink after blink, it went from unusual to worse. The monster was a deranged humanoid then a crawling, limping, tangle of wires. The monumental spider approached closer. The barbs on its legs glimmered in the lightless room. It opened its mouth wide, showcasing their sharp rows of teeth and the blots of black ink that dripped from their fangs, fangs that would have pierced Moxxi's legs had Harper and Azi not yanked them up out of harm's way. The thrust had repositioned Moxxi and brought on a moment of clarity. They were on their feet and determined, more than ever, to not let whatever this was, reach the ones who saved them.

Of all the dumb things you could have done, Moxxi . . . They warned you. You knew . . . You are an absolute idiot. They should have left you for bait. The guilt they felt was nauseating. They wanted to get control of their head. They wanted to yell and scream at what they could have possibly been thinking, but nothing could get in the way of sprinting for their life—for Azi's and Harper's life.

An argument was happening in front of them. Moxxi was only able to catch the tail end of it when Harper's black feathered hair tickled Moxxi's nose as she turned to leave.

Azi kept pulling Moxxi forward. "She's gonna bust the pipes, we gotta hide!"

Moxxi scanned the area for cover, their only light getting further and further away. "Large boxes! Over there!" Taking charge for once, they steered Azi in the right direction and lifted him atop the giant container before jumping up to join him.

Steam and water burst down the hall. Moxxi leaned around the corner to try to spot Harper. The flashlight was the only saving grace. They snatched her as soon as she came into reach.

Azi scaled up the stack of storage bins and pounded on the ceiling. A rattling resounded from his strikes and then a large clank. "Moxxi, grab that vent cover! We can climb up through here and seal the hole!"

Moxxi did as told, keeping Harper in the middle of the group. Her burns were visible, but Moxxi dared not point them out. Azi was up first, then Harper with a boost from Moxxi, and last, and probably least in their own eyes, Moxxi fumbled their way into the vent as well. Azi was ready at their side to seal the hole once everyone was accounted for, leaving the darkness behind them.

Moxxi rushed to say the words weighing on their conscience. "This is all my fault."

"It's whatever." Harper grumbled from a few feet ahead.

"It isn't. You're hurt. That's my fault."

"You didn't know." Azi reassured.

"We told them." Harper countered sharply.

"We've all been to the music room, Harps. None of us have been completely immune. It's how—" Azi tried a second time to finish his sentence. "It's how—"

"I know." Harper soothed. "But we still told them."

"You did. I should have performed better. I am fully accountable for my lack of actions." The others avoided eye contact, but Moxxi could see them nodding to themselves. "So now what? Where do we go now that we've found ourselves in the vents?"

"If things go well, we'll find the hounds." Harper encouraged.

"And if they don't?"

"Then we'll probably find out where Amari ended up." Azi added in solemnly.

Moxxi felt like that should be a good thing, like that should be what he wanted to happen more than anything, but his tone was dismal at best.

"The hounds. I cannot imagine they're like normal hounds? Relatively happy puppies with normal-sized fur and eyes and teeth?"

Harper laughed. "No. Absolutely not."

"I figured that was probably the case. This place doesn't seem to enjoy normal everyday life."

"It certainly does not." Harper flicked a dusty stick from beside her at the vent's walls. "Have you ever seen a hellhound, Moxxi?" Harper asked as if she was sure of the upcoming answer.

"Yes, actually. Often." Moxxi affirmed.

Offended that Moxxi was not taking her seriously, Harper scolded, "I'm not kidding."

"Neither am I, Harper. Most versions of hell have them, even when they're from different cultures. There's Cerberus, Garmr, black dogs, fairy hounds—"

"Are you kidding me? You say you've been around tons of hellhounds, but you can't even run a mile down a hallway?" Harper was livid.

"I did notice them twitching when they first got here. I told them if they had powers they wouldn't work here, but I was kind of joking. I meant the part after it when I asked if they were convulsing or something."

This is it. This is my chance! "I haven't been able to use any here, but I do actually tend to have some extra skills . . . powers . . . if you will."

Harper chided. "Ones that prevent you from being in shape and having to run?"

Moxxi was becoming exasperated by her constant jabs. "Yes, Harper. Even ones that prevent me from being in shape and having to run."

"Well. Okay."

"Okay?"

"Yeah. I guess so. What else do you want me to say? You claim to have powers, but admit to not being able to use them, so nothing changes right? You get to gloat and I still have to do all the work." Harper shrugged. "I think we just need to go find some hounds. No big deal for someone like you, right?"

"Sure. We can do that. No big deal." Moxxi agreed, matching Harper's challenge.

"Yeah, my dudes. No big deal." Azi agreed with an exaggerated nonchalant nature, totally oblivious to the fight surrounding him.

Part IV

They dropped into a glorious hotel lobby. A luxurious red carpet extended from the massive glass revolving doors, through an ostentatious communal area, up a wide flight of stairs, until it ultimately ended at the grand elevators in the far back of the room. The ceilings knew no bounds. The walls and floor were a cream-colored marble that sparkled with flecks of gold. Every couple of feet were chiseled pillars finer than some of the godly columns Moxxi had seen in the most prominent of underworlds. They had not known what to expect in the next section of this realm, but whatever their mind would have come up with, a gilded lobby would not have been it.

"What is this place?" Moxxi asked with as much awe as they had astonishment.

"I call this place Hotel California," Harper said as they rang a small metallic bell, shaped like an apple, at a nearby concierge stand.

"Harps has a name for everything," Azi commented. "Want to check out the treat table?" He asked waving Moxxi to join him.

"A treat table?" About halfway down the room was a thin table that spanned at least ten feet in length. Three-tiered towers of snacks lined the wall with trays of lavish sweets filling the front area, only to be end-capped by large dispensers of brightly colored drinks.

"YES! They have that orange soda you like, Harper! Come here!" Azi jumped to reach above the table for a glass, but missed. Plates of konpeitō, baklava, and tiramisu clanged against the hard floor.

Moxxi nudged a tri-colored treat with their foot and gingerly stepped through the mess to help Azi grab the cup in question. They weren't so sure about fancy pleasures in strange worlds. The five-year-old though appeared to have no inhibitions as he snatched the vessel out of their hands as soon as it was full and raced over to Harper, holding out his prize for her.

She guzzled her drink. "It's good. You should try some."

"Umm, no, thanks." Moxxi watched the two engorge themselves skeptically.

"What's up this time, Moxxi?"

"It's just—" Moxxi wasn't sure how to word their qualms. "When you talked about hellhounds, I kind of expected something a lot more—"

"Dismal? Decaying? Desolate?" Harper teased.

"Right. All that." Those were the exact words Moxxi had anticipated. "And this is . . ."

"Not always as beautiful as it appears." Harper headed a warning.

"But he's eating treats by the handful, and you're drinking that soda without any sense of concern as far as I can tell. We're all alone here, and this place is—well, it's gorgeous."

"I will give you that this particular hotel lobby has been kind to us, and a lifesaver at times when we're low on rations, but you don't always know what you're going to get here, and things hide in plain sight so you need to be careful."

"There's nothing here now." Moxxi countered.

"Oh?" Harper shined their flashlight on the far wall. Lights danced off of it in an unusual fashion. Moxxi grabbed the flashlight and walked closer. It took their eyes a while to see what was there. It was like one of those magic-eye puzzle books that kids would drop and leave in the streets of Prague. Something was there, but you had to really stare at it to see it.

"Wings. There are hundreds of wings."

"Correct." Harper walked over, took back her flashlight, and plucked one of the insects off the wall. It was there, but also not. "These are Translucent Witch Moths, or at least I think they are."

"Are they dangerous?"

"Dangerous? They're delicious!" Azi shouted with his mouth full. Bits of cookies and cream macarons escaped as he spoke.

Moxxi had a revolted look upon their face.

"That is absolutely disgusting, Azi."

"What? It was a dare!" Azi defended. "Don't knock it till you try it!"

"He also loves sardines, anchovies, and any other tin-can fish he can find. He's an eccentric kid. Giant bugs fit his vibe." Harper stated in a volume lower than what Azi could hear.

Moxxi's nausea was not subsiding with this new piece of information. "I can't believe I'm saying this, but I think I preferred talking about the evil murderous dogs."

"As you wish." Harper readjusted to have a longer conversation when Azi interrupted.

"Uhhhh. Harps." He bent down to pick something up and then walked it over to his friend.

It was a letter. Moxxi leaned over Harper's shoulder to read it with her. The words looked as if they were made out of grubby chocolate-stained fingers. *I found her. She's safe now.*

Moxxi waited for the others to speak, but when no one did, Moxxi was happy to break the silence. "That's good, right? It sounds like Gwen found Azi's sister?"

Harper clarified, "Close. That's Amari's handwriting. She must have found Gwen and left this here for us to find."

"It was right by the Taiyakis! She knows those are my favorite!"

Moxxi ignored the jubilant child for the moment and addressed the somber teen. "Harper, why aren't you happy? This sounds like incredible news, a total win!"

"If Amari has Gwen, that means that El Ojo has Gwen and despite being in this godforsaken dump for I can't even tell you how many days, we have never found that giant eye. We only know they exist because Amari was able to escape early on and told us, but that blasphemous orb made sure she would never get away again. I don't know anything about it other than it's what stole her from us."

Moxxi was speechless. Every step forward felt like it sent the group catapulting backwards. It felt hopeless after what had to be only less than a day. They couldn't imagine how these two must feel after days . . . months . . . years?

Azi elaborated. "The first time I lost her, she didn't have Brownie. I carried it everywhere with me because if you know Amari, then you know she has to have her bunny. The world stops for her if she's separated from Brownie, and her screams are worse than her nonstop crying. I don't care how evil you are, even a villain would want her to shut up after all that."

"Language, Azi."

"Sorry, Harps." He leaned over to whisper to Moxxi. "But they would. Amari could cause flooding with her tears if she wanted to, and that's the better part of her tantrums."

Moxxi was sure he was exaggerating when he spoke of his sister, but they also knew well enough not to discredit him completely. "If we get to the hounds, will they take us to El Ojo?"

"No." Harper rubbed her face. "We're going to have to go through the labyrinth."

"The labyrinth?"

Harper gestured to the elevator. "The rooms upstairs. They're pure chaos. You never know what's behind one of their doors. It could be absolutely anything: At worst, we cease to exist, and at best, we find exactly what we want. Either way, it's a lose-lose and our sole option."

"Those rooms are all death traps. We can't go up there." Azi argued.

Harper agreed. "And so is El Ojo. It's not like it's hanging out on a throne waiting for visitors to arrive. The best way to find one abomination is to go through the hive of abominations."

Moxxi noticed Azi's eyebrows beginning to furrow the way they so often did when he got emotional. They knew another fight was coming on.

"You, YOURSELF, have yelled that those rooms are off limits! 'Under no circumstances are you allowed to go there, Azi. Not even if you see Amari herself go up that elevator. Do you understand?' That's what you say to me, Harps! You say that all the time!"

"I'm the leader of this group, and I'm changing my mind! New plan! Ditch the hounds. Search the rooms. All right?"

Azi started throwing things in frustration. "NO!

NO! NO! NO! NO! You can't just change your mind and change the rules, HARPER. THIS. IS. NOT. FAIR!"

Her face was red with anger. "This is for YOUR sister! I'm risking our lives for you, AZI! I'm trying to get your family back together. Why are you throwing a tantrum over that?"

Azi was hysterical. "A TANTRUM? You think I'M throwing a tantrum? I think YOU'RE throwing a tantrum! You say you're doing this for me, for Amari, but is it for us? Or is it for Gwen? You always cared about Gwen more than Amari! I knew it! I knew you were secretly a traitor! I never should've stayed with you to begin with!" Tears were pouring down Azi's face.

That escalated quickly. Moxxi wanted to intervene, but the pair before them were feeding off of each other. Every time one exploded, the other one had to have a bigger outburst.

"I was just fine on my own! I never should've cared about two kids being lost to this place! You've been nothing but trouble since day one!"

Azi's words were no longer coherent. He was becoming a tornado of screams and projectile food.

Moxxi debated getting a word in edgewise, but feared becoming the duo's newest target of mounting wrath.

"I don't need you! I don't need any of you! I'm going to save Amari and Gwen all by myself! You'll see! Just watch what I can do without the deadweight of all of you!" Harper stomped towards the elevators with haste.

Aww, crap. I can't let her do that. Visions of tackling Harper tumbled in Moxxi's mind. Their face was set in a cringe. *I do not want to do that at all. Ughhhhh.* They called out to the tall wild-haired ball of fury, "Harper! Wait! We can talk this out!"

Harper strode towards the elevators, pounding the button to summon the mechanism down to her floor.

Moxxi swiftly jogged close behind, gingerly avoiding the mess on the floor and tried not to slip.

Then, Azi screamed a panic-stricken scream. A higher pitched, gasping, breathless scream than his previous angry screams.

Before Moxxi could even turn around, a cacophony of howls exploded in such force that the moths erupted from the safety of their wall and swirled like a hurricane around the room. The enormous bugs knocked Moxxi to their back. With some getting caught in their outfit, the insects started to drag Moxxi through the debris on the floor as they fought their way through the shirt.

Moxxi couldn't see through the layers of translucence. Everything was white and gold and distorted. Every time they struck a moth away, it would burst into a jelly-like substance. It took everything Moxxi had to not lose the contents of their stomach. They covered their mouth as they fought their way through the massive swarm.

Eww, eww, eww, eww, eww!!! I hate bugs!!

Moxxi wanted to cry but knew crying wasn't going to get them anywhere. *Think, Moxxi. Think! Quickly!* They racked their brain for what their options were. They wanted to find Harper, find Azi, and figure out what was going on with the howling beasts that had entered the room.

They didn't know how to help the others who were stuck here. Moxxi had little experience with teens, and, thankfully, even less experience with five-year-olds. *What can I do? What do I know how to do? I feel so useless here.*

Grasping at straws, they decided to focus on the noise in the room. There was so much going on, but with some determination they swore they could hear Azi yelling something in victory. *Of course, they know what to do. They planned for this. This was supposed to happen. Only an idiot wouldn't know what to do when everything goes as planned. Good for them. Now what do I do?* Moxxi pressed themself to come up with something—anything—but their mind only focused on one word and refused to let go of it. *Death. I know death.*

Resigned, Moxxi took a deep breath, closed their eyes, and began crawling towards the sounds of howls, and snarls, and growls. *I may not know how to save a human life, but I sure as heck know how to dodge the afterlife. No one's claiming these new souls but me, and I'm off duty.*

Once Moxxi set their mind to work, finding the dogs was easy. Figuring out what to do with them, was not. With hellhounds, you never quite know what you're going to get. Almost every culture has their own version of a canine death bringer, which means there's a slight variation to every beast. Moxxi had to identify them correctly before the hounds got deadly.

The growls softened as Moxxi neared the beasts, and the mass' true hellish forms displayed proudly. They were enormous in size and imposing in stature but spectral in composition. They weren't exactly translucent like the moths, but they were certainly not solid either. Moxxi didn't expect them to appear as they normally would in their respective homes; nothing here had been normal, but they did expect to be able to identify the creatures. Moxxi could spot the difference between a Black Shuck and a Moddey Dhoo with a single glance, so when they gazed upon the hotel's howling beasts of horror, their bafflement took them by surprise.

They smell like brimstone just like the Bearers of Death. But that's a snake, right? Do they have serpents protruding from their necks like Cerberus? There's their honed teeth and sharpened claws. Those parts almost look Barghest in nature. This wasn't right. *These cultures wouldn't willingly align like this. These hounds aren't configured properly.*

Flustered, and slightly indignant, Moxxi needed to know the source of these creatures. They approached one that was sequestered off to the side. Slow in their approach, Moxxi quickly, and indirectly, noted the fire in the canine's eyes along with its fanged greeting. “What happened to you?” Moxxi asked with more pain in their voice than intended.

The dog snapped their jaw at Moxxi, trying to align their blazing red eyes to their prey’s gaze, but Moxxi knew the game. It was the same no matter the origin. One could stare at the dog’s body, but never truly their eyes. Somewhere between a single fixed glance and a trio of glances, Moxxi’s soul would no longer be something they could claim as their own.

As the distance between Moxxi and the hound diminished, the beast's defensive stature was unmistakable. It was very aware of Moxxi’s presence, but it did not give chase. It did not pursue. It waited, bracing for their intruder to draw closer. In the decades Moxxi had spent transporting souls from one underworld to the next, a hellhound only remained still under one condition: It was guarding something.

Positive of their conviction, they held their focus while hoping the others were handling themselves well. *If I can figure this out, maybe we all stand a chance.* The hound’s body was haunched as Moxxi drew near, eager to ignite a final-blow. Moxxi trusted their instincts and let their focal point pivot from the imminent threat in front of them, to what lay just beyond the obvious line of sight. At first, it looked like a simple shadow: thin, crisp, stable, and an impressively dark hunter-green. *Green? Why is that green?* Moxxi circled around the hellhound for a better view, sure to stay outside of biting range. They began to smell something more than brimstone. They began to smell moss and must. A breeze of chilled air crossed Moxxi's face. The former shadow replicated a glimpse into a calm night sky, and, if turned just right, an exceedingly pointed nose.

Moxxi's mouth fell agape. They had heard stories of the Mother of Hounds since their creation, but had never come across her. Matilda of the Night was an old crone with spectral fiendish monstrosities at her beck and call. *But didn't she have a partner? And ride in the night sky? Didn't she chase lost souls? Why would you be here?* "Mallt-y-Nos?"

A sneer formed in the starlit façade, and then it was gone. Whomever the crone was, was no longer. Unfortunately, Moxxi realized a moment too late that this also meant the former guard dog had been relieved of its guarding duties.

A loud gnash of teeth sounded at Moxxi's side, and they used every ounce of energy they had to run. Obscenities blared in their head. They mentally kicked themself. They knew better than to be an Icarus in a strange world. They should have been more strategic in their actions. Death was only one mistake away, and they were no longer safe behind Morse-made barriers.

The moths had mostly been cleared out of the room which left the floors slick with goo. More dogs joined the pack of Moxxi's aggressor and flanked the charcoal hound in its pursuit. Moxxi's luck was running out. They were grateful they weren't surrounded, but they needed to find a way out of here. With an inability to think clearly, they followed the last good plan they heard and hoped getting to the elevator would be enough. Harper and Azi came into view as Moxxi neared the wide staircase. They swore they even saw a brief expression of relief on Harper's face when they locked eyes.

"To the elevators!" Moxxi called out with the little air they had left in their lungs.

Harper must have heard because she pushed Azi up the stairs as she protected them with her trusty flashlight from the lunging jaws in front of them.

Why is she using a flashlight in a well-lit room and how is that actually working? The thought distracted Moxxi and an aggressive chomp pierced their ankle. They fell face first on the marble staircase. The crunch of their nose echoed in their ears. Two hands grabbed the collar of Moxxi's shirt and began to pull. A ding sounded from behind them, and with a hefty thrust, Moxxi found themself sitting in the base of the elevator, their friends at their side, and a large pack of ghastly, gruesome, hounds staring at them as the doors closed.

Why are they just sitting there? Moxxi eyed the beasts skeptically.

At that moment, Moxxi realized everything had worked as planned. The three of them had been trapped with nowhere else to go but up. The doors latched firmly, and they rode deeper into the heart of this wretched world.

Part V

The elevator chimed, signaling that the trio had reached their destination. In any other circumstance, this hallway would be considered dull and boring. Another lush red carpet lined the walkway, and at the far end was a small table with a pair of flowers on it. A large mirror stared back at the disheveled group. Moxxi watched their reflection long enough to wonder if their counterparts heard the noise but quickly realized they were simply doing the same thing Moxxi was: stalling. Eventually, Harper broke the statuesque stalemate. Azi was the next to exit, and Moxxi headed up the rear, feeling more comfortable that they could ensure no one was left behind.

With all the desired visitors delivered as intended, the doors of the elevator collided behind the kids, making them jump. Where the metal contraption once stood, the space now resembled a boring regular wall that mimicked the one on the opposing end. The room was now perfectly symmetrical.

"Not that we intended to go back, but it's worth noting that that option is no longer available," Moxxi evaluated, pressing onto the freshly formed structure.

"I'm not surprised. Leaving opportunities for escape isn't El Ojo's favorite pastime."

"What is their favorite then, Harps?" Azi wandered down the long hall, getting close, but not too close, to the five doors on the left side of the space. He alternated muttering Amari's and Gwen's names as he passed each entryway. When he reached the final door, he looked back to his friends. "What will El Ojo do to them?"

His tone was more inquisitive and less distraught than Moxxi anticipated him to sound.

"I'm not sure, buddy." Harper sat down at the base of the red carpet. "I hope, for everyone's sake, nothing that makes life harder than it already is."

Azi continued to question the situation. "Is that what happened last time? Did life get harder?"

Moxxi's ears perked at the question. *Last time?*

Harper shot an annoyed look at the boy that gave "That's not your business to bring up now, is it?" vibes.

He didn't even make eye contact. He was lost in his own thoughts.

Sighing, Harper gave in. "I would say so. Everyone but me went up the elevator, and no one came back down for . . . days? Weeks? I hope I wasn't a sucker enough to wait around for any longer than that."

"Harper!" The words left Moxxi's lips without any planned follow-up questions.

The two others turned in surprise towards Moxxi.

"You lost your entire troupe and didn't mention anything until now?"

"I told the kid not to come up here! What more do you want from me?"

Moxxi was aghast. They knew Harper had good intentions, and probably knew The Backrooms more comprehensively than anyone else in the group, but that didn't change the fact that she was leading them all straight into their own demise. "When were you going to tell us that the people that used to be bonded with you, all died here? That's huge information to just casually drop!"

Harper grumbled under her breath. "We don't know that they died."

Moxxi could barely hear her through their own thoughts. "What are you even saying?" Moxxi criticized.

"We don't KNOW that they're dead . . ." Harper repeated disdainfully.

"Oh, really? You think they just came up to this creepy hotel hallway after leaving those yellow-colored hunting grounds and what? What do you think, Harper? You think they just went on living their best and happiest lives? That we'll open the door to a field and all of your former friends will be happily frolicking among the wildflowers asking where you've been this whole time?" Moxxi's words were more heated than they intended, but anger was flowing through them. "How dare you risk our lives and not tell us!"

"I TOLD HIM!" Harper stood and pointed sharply at Azi. "I told him over and over and over again and that was all fine until YOU came here!"

"I'm here to HELP you!"

Harper laughed in Moxxi's face. "I can see that! With your inability to run, to be silent, or to pull up your own body, how could I miss all the great help you bestow upon us? My apologies, great one. I was a fool to have missed your contributions up to this point. I—"

"—STOP!" Azi's face was red and tear streaked.

No one had paid any mind to him while they were fighting. They hadn't noticed he was no longer in the middle of the carpet. They hadn't noticed that he had opened a door. They hadn't noticed him failing to muster enough strength to shove the door closed in order to keep what looked to be a grown man's arm out.

"Disguiser!" Harper yelled, jolting forward.

Moxxi joined in too. With the three of them working together, the door closed as the monster shrieked in the background. A soft plop muffled out the creature's cries, and something wet and heavy fell on Moxxi's feet. They turned their face toward the ceiling. "If I turn around and there's a dismembered arm on my shoe, I am not going to be okay."

"Wimp." Harper whispered into Moxxi's ear as she tickled their face with an extra-large moth wing.

Relief overcame them. "That was not what I expected that to be."

"I think she ate him," Azi commented while watching Harper tease his friend.

"You ate a Disguiser?" Moxxi asked Harper, increasingly perplexed.

"Not me, dummy. This moth." She wiggled the wing at her side. "He thinks the Witch Moth ate the Disguiser."

"Oh." That probably made more sense. "Did it?" Moxxi had no idea how that would work.

Harper shrugged. "If she were big enough, anything is possible. However, if the moth can eat an entity that is the size of a full-grown adult, what do we think it can do to little boys who make ill-advised decisions?" She bonked him on the head with the insect's remains. "Hmm?"

"You two weren't doing nothing! Well, nothing but fighting! We're here to find Gwen and Amari, not bicker about all your friends dying."

Harper was taken aback and bit her lips to prevent saying something she regretted.

Moxxi interjected. "While that's true, Azi, I've been surrounded by death my entire creation, and I have yet to find someone that recommends it. I'd much rather you kick me in the shins than open another door by yourself, is that a fair trade?"

His eyes grew wide, and a mischievous smile spread across his face. He looked like a kid who just successfully got away with something naughty. His words came out in a whisper obstructed with not-so-subtle giggles. "I can kick you? Really? You mean it?"

They didn't. They hadn't meant to be taken literally, but for some reason they were finding it hard to say that out loud. "If the only options left in the world are to kick me or open a door leading to your imminent death, then yes, please come kick me instead."

"Okay! Want to go back to fighting with Harps then? She was saying—"

"Ah ah ah, little one! We'll not be having that!" Harper scolded gently.

Azi huffed. "She always ruins everything . . ." He paused, then looked up to Moxxi with hope in his voice, ". . . doesn't that make you a little mad?"

"Unfortunately, it does not." Moxxi clarified.

Azi groaned. "Whatever then." He kicked the previously opened door. "Sorry if all your friends died, too."

"What?" Moxxi didn't expect that and wasn't sure where that came from.

"You said you were always surrounded by death. Doesn't that mean you also have no friends? Just like Harps?"

Harper rubbed her temples as she listened to Azi's form of support.

"You are right that I have no friends, but they did not die," Moxxi answered, giving Harper a little wink.

"It's just no one likes you?" Azi continued.

Harper had to control herself not to scold him again, but Moxxi's outstretched hand promised that they knew what they were doing.

"That's exactly it. No one likes me. I'm a foul, awful person, and therefore, I have no friends."

Azi laughed. "I can see it." He nodded eagerly.

Moxxi feigned heartbreak.

"I'm just kidding! I don't not like you," Azi complimented.

"And you?" Moxxi prodded Harper with their foot.

"I don't not like you either," Harper reassured.

"Well, there we have it then. We all don't not like each other. Which means no dying. We all survive together, so we all open doors together. Agreed?"

"Agreed," the other two said in unison.

Pleased to have a win, Moxxi continued, "I think the next door we choose, we should all choose together."

"Or maybe we could take turns. I did one, then Harper can do one, then you can Moxxi," Azi suggested.

"Sounds like a fine plan, young sir." Moxxi switched to address Harper. "Which one next, Captain? By my count we have at least nine other ways to find bad things. What's your pick?"

Harper rolled her eyes. She was not a fan of Moxxi becoming likable. "I've always liked the number three."

"Three is a good number," Moxxi encouraged. "Which door should we count as one?"

Azi was the first to answer. "How about the first one I opened is the first door?"

"I can live with that. Do we count all up one side? Making this left side one through five? Or is it more of an even and odds thing?"

"Evens and odds! Evens and odds!" He cheered.

Harper stepped to the side and leaned her back against the next door. "Then this makes three."

Azi confirmed her thoughts. "It does! What do you think it'll be? The last one was a boring old cave. Lame."

Moxxi shook their head. "Lame is definitely what I think of when I think of that disgusting arm trying to pull you to your doom. How boring!" Their words were drowning in snark.

Harper caught Moxxi's attention before proceeding. She spoke in a tone lower than Azi's cheers. "I like boring. I miss boring. I want this one to be even more boring."

Moxxi had heard those same words from souls they had transported. At the end of the day, everyone seemed to want a simple life, and Moxxi knew that plan was already a failed one if they were involved. No use dulling Harper's spirits, though. Sarcasm was going to have to do. "Impending doom, here we come?" Moxxi offered before bracing for the horrors of their next encounter.

"Impending doom, indeed." Harper repeated, resigned to her fate ahead.

"Woohoo! Let's do it! Impending doom!" Azi shouted gleefully.

Part VI

The air was heavy with salt. The walls of the room were gray and the room was furnished just as you could expect someone's living room to look, with a few exceptions. The disjointment here revolved around the floor. This room was entirely flooded. Broken boards floated atop a dark murky water, bumping into things as they went. While there were ordinary bookshelves and a mundane mantle, there was also a tilted couch blocking the entryway to the next part of the house. Moxxi assumed that as it had begun to float away, it had gotten lodged inside the wooden frame.

"It smells like the ocean." Azi observed, leaning further into the room than Moxxi would have liked.

"I don't see any shark fins. That has to be a good sign, right?" Moxxi tried to remain hopeful of their perilous predicament.

Harper was having none of it. Her mind was on pure strategy. "I'll jump first, I guess. I think I can make it to the couch if I stick my landings well enough. I'll try to straighten the couch too, so then we can all fit." Moxxi gave her a thumbs up as she bent her knees, swung her arms, and hyped herself up. Harper let out a loud exhale as she landed on a table even with the water's surface.

"Wow. She's so cool," Azi said to no one in particular.

Moxxi was starting to feel the same. They hadn't even seen that spot as a possible landing option.

With another leap, Harper was scaling a bookshelf, climbing her way across it like a spider monkey. With her superior agility, she balanced perfectly on the frame of the perpendicular couch. She held onto its top armrest, and slid her feet to stand on the bottom one. She rocked her body hard to dislodge the couch from the arched doorway.

"Use your BUTT!" Azi called from the safety point.

Harper looked at him in disapproving surprise.

Azi was adamant in his recommendation, pointing to his bottom and wiggling it towards his trusted companion. "It helps! You can push lots of things with your butt! I'm not even making a fart joke! That's how serious I am!"

Moxxi covered their face to hide their smile. They may not have the closeness of a sibling relationship with Azi, but they had no doubts that the time they had spent with him since arriving in The Backrooms was exactly how it would feel to have a younger brother. They understood why Gwen would go after him once she found out he was missing from camp.

"It worked! TOLD YOU!" Azi gloated.

In the time Moxxi had spent in their thoughts, Harper had handled the couch situation and was testing to see if it would function as a boat if she used her hands to paddle. It did. She grabbed a fire poker from the mantle, stabbed some loose boards at an angle, and once she had a sufficient stack, she pushed her way back to her friends.

"I'll jump next!" Azi leapt without concern and missed the table by several feet.

"You're all wet now!" Harper complained as she pulled him onto their makeshift watercraft.

The child, clearly embarrassed, climbed up half-heartedly onto the couch. "That's a lot harder than it looks! I bet you'll fall right in, too." He judged crabbily at Moxxi.

If this situation had presented itself a few days ago, Moxxi would have ignored Azi and climbed onto the couch that Harper was clearly navigating over to them, so there would be no risk involved. They eyed the water then up to Harper, gesturing for thoughts on their next move. Harper didn't say no, so Moxxi did what they felt was the right call for morale.

They closed the hotel door behind them, plugged their nose and stepped right into the murkiness below. When they bobbed back up to the surface and were able to climb onto the safety vessel, it was impossible not to see Azi's glow. All his embarrassment was gone, and he had a pillow in hand ready to offer Moxxi a way to dry off.

"Are we done then?" Harper chaffed.

"You look out of place. Do you feel left out?" Moxxi splashed water on their dry counterpart.

"I do not." Harper's conviction was solid. "Now that we have picked a door, let's see where we ended up, especially since you two have successfully made your way to the couch in the most efficient manner."

"Yes. Onward, Captain!" Moxxi goaded.

"Ay Ay Cap-i-tan!" Azi embellished.

The couch steered easily and steadily on the water. There was no current, no waves, and no surprise visitors from down below. Moxxi began to think maybe the house was just severely flooded, and the rest of the world would be normal until Azi tugged on their clothes to direct their attention out the large window in the kitchen area.

"It looks like it smells," He said matter-of-factly.

"And what's that like?" Harper asked without needing to see what he was focusing on.

"Like the ocean. This whole place smells like the ocean."

Harper anticipated his response. "That's a good thing for you, isn't it? You love the ocean."

"I do . . ." he agreed tentatively.

Moxxi thought it was a nice place to end up as well. "I just saw the ocean for the first time right before I came here. It's very pretty, but can also be kind of scary if you overthink it."

Azi's emotions burst to the surface. "I think so too! A monster could just swim right up and chomp off your toes, and you'd never see it coming!"

"Are you worried about a monster eating your toes right now?" Harper was steady in her inquiry.

Azi was silent and thought for a while. "No. No, I don't think I am."

"Then I think that's a win." Harper jiggled a door in front of her. "A little help please?"

Azi, without anyone asking him to, jumped into the water and pulled on the medium sized oak door in front of them. It glided open easily, once the couch was out of its path.

Moxxi reached down, ready to pull the boy up, as Harper navigated them outside the house. The sun was present, but offered no warmth. It cast a dim shadowy light over the infinite sea before them. The water was slightly brighter out here; instead of looking blackish in color, it was now a dusty sea of brownish-gray. Its gloomy horizon did not provide any sense of direction. The world here was monotonous.

"Do you guys see . . . anything?" Moxxi wasn't sure what they wanted to find, but a never-ending stretch of nothingness was not their top pick.

"No, but that means no entities either, and I'll take that."

"Yeah. Let's keep going." Azi sounded half in thought.

They went for what felt like hours like that: wordless and rowing into oblivion. Harper never said a word, but Moxxi knew she had to be exhausted.

"Want to switch?" Moxxi recommended.

Harper looked around the ocean, even the house they were in earlier was no longer in view. Nothing was in view. "I suppose that's fine."

Moxxi took the spot at the front of the couch. "You struggle with sharing responsibilities, especially if that means letting someone else lead."

Harper's defenses instantly rose. "That's certainly a weird way to say, 'Thanks for all your hard work, Harper.'"

Moxxi stopped pushing the makeshift boat. "I didn't mean it like that, okay? I just meant that keeping us all safe seems really important to you, and that must be much harder to do if someone else is at the helm of things."

Harper wasn't thrilled with the intended meaning either. "I can't push us along all night. We'd have to take turns eventually. Steering a boat is a lot harder than turning on a flashlight."

"I couldn't believe that worked in a well-lit room earlier."

Harper pulled out her trusted device and flipped it on, inches away from Moxxi's face.

"Ow! What the heck?"

"It hurt, didn't it?" Harper verified.

"That would be why I said 'ow.' Little rude of you, don't you think?"

"It hurts their eyes more." Harper concluded.

Moxxi felt deflated as they paddled. They just wanted to have some small talk. Refusing to look back, they traveled onwards and kept to themself. No birds cawed, no wind blew, the sun never moved. Moxxi's internal clock suspected that it had to be night time, or day time, by now, but the sky was unchanged. Moxxi was ready to break the silence and try, once again, to talk to Harper, but when they turned, she instantly put her finger up to her lips.

Moxxi's first reaction was that they were under attack, but after a second of observation it was actually a sleeping Azi in Harper's lap that invoked the request. *It must be something to feel safe enough to lay on another like that. Or to have someone choose you so definitively.* The concept was foreign to Moxxi but pulled at their heart. *It looks nice, peaceful even.* They didn't want to spoil the moment.

Careful not to wake the boy up, Moxxi sat on the couch next to Harper, whispering in a soft enough volume not to disturb his peace. "The sun is still in the same position as it was when we first arrived. Isn't that strange?"

"I had that thought too. Azi's stomach has been grumbling as well. It must have been hours since he gorged himself on sweets in the hotel lobby."

"Do you have any food left in your backpack?"

"It's probably crushed, but some."

Moxxi smirked at a memory. "From all your glute work earlier?"

Harper's face blanched. "The hounds weren't necessarily delicate in their advance, but yes, taking Azi's suggestion with the couch didn't help any. I should've opted for less destructive tactics."

"Nah. You kept the kid safe and made him happy. I'm pretty sure that's what you are supposed to do. His giggles are worth their weight in gold." Moxxi resisted the urge to play with his hair while he slept.

"Not just me. I doubt you jumped into the unknown waters because you love sitting for hours in wet clothes."

"I don't know. You hate all of my decision making, maybe that's just another flaw to add to the pile."

"I do not!" Harper guffawed.

Moxxi gave her a sideways glare.

"I don't hate EVERYTHING."

Moxxi dramatized their glare.

"I'm sure you ate food in the lobby that was totally reasonable. You said no to the moth wing. That's at least one point there."

Moxxi hadn't eaten from the treat buffet, but they didn't want to talk on that topic. "I did say no to the moth wing."

"See? Point proven."

If you only knew my eating habits, I doubt you'd agree with those either.

"Plus, it's not like you're my biggest fan either, Moxxi. You get plenty irritated when you're talking to me."

They were dumbfounded. “Why would you say that?”

“The constant arguing is typically a good clue.” Harper said with snark.

“I’m not trying to be difficult. I apologize for that.” Moxxi truly didn’t dislike Harper and was sad that it came across that way. “I do think you’re a bit . . . hardened. But I also consider that to be a product of your circumstances. Losing your whole team and then leading a new one that consists of two small humans cannot be an easy task for a teen.”

“It’s not, but that doesn't mean there’s another option.” Harper laughed to herself. “You know, I don’t know the last time someone called me a teen. How old do you think I am, Moxxi?”

Guessing someone’s age felt like a trap, but Moxxi led with honesty. “You look slightly younger than me. I’d guess you were around seventeen.”

“I do think we’re very similar in age, but, no offense, I doubt your appearance matches your actual age. You don’t seem like someone born near me. Not in the way Azi, or Amari, or my previous team was.”

“When were you born?”

“1983: the era of big hair, tacky workout clothes, and even worse music.”

“Take that back! I love 80s music!”

“Because it’s so vintage?” Her mockery of the last word impersonated criticisms she received over the years.

“I suppose I was around for some of it.”

"And earlier than that?"

Moxxi focused on the stillness of the water. "You're going to think I'm being difficult again."

Harper bumped Moxxi's shoulder with her own. "Tis the way, right?"

Moxxi smiled. "It seems so. Umm, I don't really know. I'm not totally sure when I was created."

"You keep using that word. It's off putting. Why can't you say born or birthed if you're determined to be unconventional."

Moxxi knew the answer to that question, but wasn't sure if Harper wanted to.

"You're giving me a strange look. Do you not know who your mom is?"

That was an easy one. "I do not."

"Wow. I'm sorry. What about your dad?"

This was not as easy. Moxxi knew Mors had created them when they were tired of patrolling and were ready to hand off their duties to a chosen heir. They also knew that while Mors mostly chose their male form, their name had feminine roots, and while that opened up many options for creating a descendant of their own, it only complicated the situation for Moxxi. The only thing Moxxi knew for sure was that Mors was there to give them work, and that was it. Their relationship, if you could even call it that, consisted of absolutely nothing else. All Moxxi would ever be to them is a worker bee made to relieve the stress of his, or her, daily tasks.

"It's okay not to answer. Families can be tough

sometimes."

"I imagine so. Did you get along with yours?"

Harper shook her head. "No. Not really. I mean, I knew who my parents were, but they didn't get me. I felt like I was always letting them down, and I hated that feeling. A lot."

"I can verify that it does indeed suck to feel like you're coming up short on things."

"I didn't mean—"

"I know, but it's true. I'm used to being by myself, being able to handle anything that needs to be handled, and I can't even perform basic endurance tests here. It's incredibly infuriating."

"Like death?" Harper's tone perked at the end of her sentence, trying to use a throwback from their earlier conversation.

"Like death," Moxxi said with absolute confidence.

"Azi said you were trying to summon powers when we were back at the hideout."

"He did."

"Was he right?" Curiosity had gotten the best of her, but Harper countered instantly, "Unless you don't want to answer. Which is totally fair and reasonable."

Maybe if there had been tension in their talks, maybe if Azi's energy was distracting their focus, maybe if Moxxi hadn't felt so lonely out here at sea, their answer would have been different. "He caught me trying to turn into a shadow. I move much faster in that form, and as you have so graciously pointed out, many times, I could use the agility booster."

Harper's eyes were wide with astonishment. "For real? You can do that?"

Moxxi nodded.

"That's so cool. Anything else?"

"I also usually have a torch with me. That helps guide me, literally and metaphorically, to where I need to go."

"Whoa. I don't have anything like that."

"I don't think you need anything else. You're exceptionally talented just as you are."

"Not like that. All I can do is barely survive."

"That's more than me." Moxxi playfully ribbed.

"If you can't survive, then what can you do?" Harper was trying to piece together the clues they'd been given.

"I can transport."

"Transport?"

"Yup. I can take people from one place to the next and promise a safe delivery to wherever it is that they need to go."

"Oh." Harper was quiet, breaking the flow of exchanges. "I see."

Do you? Moxxi didn't want to come off rude, so they let their thoughts stay inside their mind.

"Like, in death, right? That's what you're trying to say? People die, and then you turn into a shadow and use your torch and take them . . . places?" Harper was on the brink of understanding.

"That is mostly correct, yes."

"You're like a Grim Reaper?"

"If I were Christian, I suppose I would be."

"What are you?"

There were so many ways Moxxi could answer that. "In terms of lineage? Roman."

"I see." The weight of Harper's words was unmistakable. "If you're not a reaper, but you still take people . . . places . . . where do you take them?"

This was a question all humans asked. Time and time again, everyone was always the same. "I take them wherever they need to go." Moxxi was resolute in their delivery. It was a well-practiced response.

"Then . . ." Harper was flustered. ". . . then are we not dead? I seriously thought we were all dead here."

Moxxi was taken aback. They had never given that idea a second's thought. "No, Harper. You're not dead. I came here through some bad dreams. Admittedly, they were not mentally sound, but this isn't death, this is something mimicking the dream world, an alternate reality of some kind."

"A dream." Harper's tone was full of spite. "More like an endless nightmare."

Part VII

The sea was wearisome, drab, and endless. Moxxi was not surprised that once Harper had stopped chatting, she had fallen asleep, slumped on top of Azi. Moxxi would need sleep too, eventually. Their body was starting to feel heavy and sluggish. It had been an exasperating amount of time in this realm. Monsters, angst, and emotions ran high here.

To counter the trying times, Moxxi replayed happy memories in their mind. They thought of times that made them feel powerful. They yearned to feel strong again and shake off the increasing shame of not being as tactical as their ego believed they should be. They were ready to be out of this place and have their life go back to normal. *Maybe returning to Prague wouldn't be that bad after all*, they mused, barely noticing their eyelids slowly drooping.

Moxxi's dreams were quiet. Not only did no one ask for help or guidance or answers to questions Moxxi had no idea of, but there were no souls to be found. It was as if that part of Moxxi, too, had been stifled. Though, at this point, Moxxi was not complaining about having less demands being thrown in their lap.

They cruised the dream plane seamlessly, conjuring up their own spacious and glorious yacht, bobbing along a perfectly gentle sea, a bright warm sun, and their feet dangling in the water. A large sea turtle swam underneath their toes. The beauty that was created by the sun and water dancing upon the turtle's shell was majestic. The creature was astonishing. Not only was it the epitome of longevity, its movements were soothing and perfectly in tune with the ocean around it. Moxxi couldn't resist swaying along with its loops and twirls. They debated going into the water with the creature for a closer look, but were jostled awake by a harsh cry.

"KA-KA-KA!"

Moxxi's eyes shot open. A mighty bird stood in Azi's spot. *What in the world?* It looked similar to a crane, but Moxxi had never seen one of such magnitude before. They reached over and shook Harper awake. Flummoxed how she could sleep through such a thing, Moxxi was urgent in their physical plea. *She is not going to be happy if Azi turned into a bird.* Harper opened her eyes slowly, but Moxxi could feel her body jump once she caught sight of the bird.

"KA-KA-KA!"

Harper gazed wide-eyed at Moxxi. Moxxi nodded. Neither of them spoke.

"KA-KA-KA!"

Just then, a colossal animal rose from the sea. It was as dark as a night sky with beaming white spots. Its width surpassed the couch's three-fold as it rose to the edge of the surface. Its mouth was a terrifying gaping hole, comparable to the cyclones Moxxi had seen ravage people's nightmares. When Moxxi was sure the next chapter within this realm was going to be encapsulated within the belly of this gilled leviathan, the tail of the massive beast flicked up behind the creature, and the air was filled with an eruption of giggles from Azi.

"KA-KA—"

"—enough!" Moxxi shouted in frustration to the aviary nuisance before turning to the gleeful five-year-old. "Azi! What in the world are you doing?" Moxxi resisted their urge to yell at the child that this thing, whatever it is, could fit an entire house in their maw so perhaps he shouldn't play on its tail!

"Moxxi! You're awake!" The child cheered.

Harper peeked her head over the brim of the couch, side-eyeing the human-sized bird beside her, and in a low voice growled, "Get. Out. Of. The. Water. Azi."

"You two are such grumps! I'm not leaving. Come play!"

Moxxi didn't know the words to tell them that any of these things could lead to his end, and he needed to listen first and ask questions later.

Tiny bubbles, all in a line, were approaching from the side. Moxxi couldn't tell if they were headed towards Azi or the couch, and Moxxi wasn't going to give the unknown source enough time to find out. Confident the mouth of the midnight beast was behind them, they drove towards the small boy, with no abilities to protect him other than their determination.

As Moxxi fought to scoop him up, losing to his resistance, the beast's tail began to swish. It wasn't aggressive, but it didn't have to be. The two-foot tall waves were more than enough to carry Moxxi far out of reach from Azi. They were more than enough to distance Harper, and the couch, from Azi too.

It's separating us. We'll be easier to pick off if we're not together. Moxxi tried to fight the waves, but their strength was miniscule in comparison. A hardened platform swept them up from behind. Instinctively, Moxxi glanced down, trying to steady themself on the moving surface. A familiar shell shone below them, and the sea turtle from their dreams met their gaze.

"Ha! See! You think you can boss me around because you're older, but you don't stand a chance against Ebisu!" Azi admonished.

"Ebisu? What's an Ebisu?" Moxxi shouted from a far distance.

"That's the name of this whale shark! They told me no one would take me away from them unless I wanted them to and they were right! You lose, Moxxi!"

That thing talks? Moxxi wasn't a fan of this revelation.

"KA-KA-KA!" The bird stretched from its position, flexing its wings to their full length. They were only a third of Ebisu's size but nonetheless, remained incredibly intimidating. Their talons latched onto the arm of the couch, they stretched their neck outwards, and then they started flying Harper back to her original position as well.

Strange. Why is it doing that? Why are they gathering us? Moxxi speculated.

The crane flew faster than the turtle swam. Harper reached Azi first. He still refused to climb on the couch, but in Harper's new position, he sat at the base of the structure next to the whale shark's dorsal fin. Moxxi's transportation delivered them close, but it was impossible to get back to their seat without touching the gigantic fish.

"If I accidentally touch them, are they going to eat me?" Moxxi didn't quite mean to say that aloud, but it was a significant concern for them.

"What? No!" Azi answered incredulously. "Whale sharks eat plankton. Don't you know anything?"

Not even a little bit. I thought that much was clear. Moxxi was bending at weird angles to avoid touching the navy-blue surface just below their feet. Harper helped them up once they were in reach.

Moxxi gestured to the bird. "I see you made a new friend?"

"I guess so?" Harper replied hesitantly. "But this place isn't really known for providing friends."

"What even is it?" Moxxi questioned.

"I think it's a crane?" Harper informed.

"Yeah. That's Fukurokuju. He's noisy, but he's a good guy. He's holding Daikokuten, I don't think the little mouse swims really well."

What are these words this kid is saying? Has he lost his mind?

Harper stroked the crane's head cautiously. He leaned in and a little shimmy went down his body. A mouse peeked out from the plumage of the bird's chest. Startled, Harper froze. The tiny rodent handed her an even tinier radish. She didn't move.

Azi hush-yelled at her. "Take it, Harper. Don't be rude."

Stunned, she willed her to close her hand and push gratitude out of her mouth. "Thank you."

This is weird, even for me. Moxxi looked for their turtle companion. They were chilling behind the couch, relaxed as ever. "Okay. So. The big thing is Ebisu. The noisy thing is Fukurokuju, and the small mouse hiding in him is Daikokuten."

"Slightly rude, but yes," Azi remarked condescendingly.

"Then, what's this one's name?" Moxxi pointed over to their sea friend who was now eating a jellyfish. *Where in this world did it find that?*

"That's also Fukurokuju . . ." Azi explained, expecting pushback.

The turtle slapped his fin on the water. Moxxi bent over the piece of furniture to see what was wrong. Marine Fukurokuju was shaking his head with intent. Moxxi leaned over further to reach him.

I hope that jellyfish didn't hurt him. Once Moxxi was close enough, the sea creature plopped the remains of his dinner in their hand, headbutted Moxxi's fingers closed then submerged back into the sea. Moxxi's stomach wretched.

"KA-KA-KA!" Everyone looked to the aviary Fukurokuju. The mouse let out a loud squeak from his hiding place, and then, the whale shark started to bob and weave.

Azi cried out. "NO!"

Harper reached out for the boy. "Azi, what's wrong?"

The crane lifted up off the sofa and soared high into the sky.

Sullen, Azi took Harper's hand. "He says they have to go now." He looked away as the whale shark disappeared within the murky depths below.

Why would they leave so soon? Moxxi judged. "Didn't they just get here?"

"No. But I still don't want them to go." Azi pouted.

"They just came out like ten minutes ago."

"That's when you woke up. They were here like . . ." Irritated, Azi counted. ". . . like five hours while you two slept all your life away."

Moxxi didn't love his tone, but they knew he was upset so they held their tongue. They also highly doubted they slept for five hours after the quartet of animals arrived.

Azi pulled his body as far away as he could from the others. “This is stupid. Everything that feels like home leaves.”

His last sentence felt heavy to Moxxi. Feeling abandoned was something they understood well. They wanted to comfort the child, despite having little practice at such a task. “It must be incredibly hard to miss home and know that anytime you get a glimpse of it, whatever joy you find never sticks around.”

He glared at Moxxi. “Yeah. Obviously.”

Harper readjusted herself. “All right. I think it’s my turn to paddle.”

Moxxi didn’t feel like they were all ready to leave yet. It didn’t feel right to sweep Azi’s feelings under the rug and just keep on keeping on. “Would you like to steer us for a while, Azi? If we’re lucky, maybe we’ll come across something that feels good again?” This wasn’t within Moxxi’s power to offer, but they ignored that fact.

“Really?” Azi wanted validation from Harper.

She smiled and snickered in a low voice, “You can’t do a worse job than they did, right?”

He grinned like the five-year-old he deserved to be.

Feigning offense, Moxxi called them out. “I can hear you all talking about me!”

Harper winked at them and reached for the paddle.

“What’s that?” Azi asked, pointing to Harper’s

hand.

She turned her palm over to show the radish the mouse had given her. It was now a golden mallet.

Sharing the same surprise as Harper, Moxxi repeated her action. A multi-pointed object with smooth tips glowed in their hand. When they picked it up, they realized a thin, shiny chain was attached to it.

Azi's face was enamored. "Put it on! Put it on!!"

Moxxi checked in with Harper with their eyes. When she didn't disagree, Moxxi draped the necklace around their neck and clasped it shut.

"It's mesmerizing," Harper complimented.

"He did good with that one," Azi affirmed.

"I thought it was jellyfish guts?" Moxxi cringed.

Harper held out their gift. "I thought mine was a radish."

"What do you think yours does?" Moxxi wondered.

"I have absolutely no idea." Harper reflected. "Did they tell you anything, Azi?"

He shook his whole body from side to side with a flare of silliness. "Nope. All I got were a few cans of tin fish. Want some?" He cracked open a metal parcel. It had a distinguished smell.

Oh, eww. That is pungent. Moxxi tried to control their facial reaction.

Azi waved the aroma to his nose. "Yum! Red snapper! Delicious! If you want one, you ought to take it now because I'm about to eat this WHOLE thing! I'm STARVING." He held the container across Harper's body, bumping Moxxi's arm with his hand.

A fog cleared in their brain. *Ame.*

"Moxxi, hello?? Can you please make a decision about the fish?" Harper pleaded. "They are very close to my face."

"You can have some too, Harps. I wasn't only offering it to Moxxi."

"I know. I think I'm good. Thanks."

He rolled his eyes. "You never know what's good for you." Getting impatient, he bumped them again. "Moxxi!"

Yomi. Kami. "Kami?" They responded.

"Kami? Red snapper." He corrected.

"No. Ame. Yomi. Kami." *Those are all Shinto locations and forces.*

"You're creeping me out, Mox," Harper warned.

Moxxi tried to straighten out their thoughts and their brain. "Azi, does your family descend from Shinto beliefs?"

"I don't know nothing about that," He asserted with a mouth full of snapper.

"It's a belief system mostly located in Japan."

"Oh! Japan! Yeah. My family is from Japan. Well, my mom is anyway. Why? What's that mean to you?"

"It means . . ." Moxxi was putting it all together. "It means I have at least one of my powers back."

Part VIII

"Hey, look!" Azi smacked his lips together, chomping down on his canned fish.

Moxxi squinted. "I don't see anything."

The boy picked up the paddle and pointed with it. "That! Over there!"

"I can get us there if you want! I'd much rather do that than keep sitting on this couch watching you eat fish." Harper wasn't thrilled with Moxxi's suggestion of letting the five-year-old act as captain, and it was showing.

"Do you see something?" Moxxi asked her quietly.

Harper's facial expression strongly implied not only did they not see anything, but they did not believe that Azi was seeing anything either.

"No! It's right there! Look!" Azi dusted off his hands on his clothes, set his favorite meal down, and took two hands to the paddle.

Moxxi was surprised how well he could manage a couch with two people double his size on it.

Harper stared forward, ready to take over if needed.

It was just a glint, but Moxxi thought the kid might actually be onto something. "Harper. There's something there." Moxxi's tone was serious.

Azi groaned in agitation. "Don't you guys LISTEN? I JUST said that!"

"There can't be. There's nothing here." Hope was at the edge of Harper's voice.

"I know. I know. I thought this place was an abandoned pit too, but seriously, it almost looks like there's a speck of something out there." Moxxi was eager to find any leverage point. They surmised even a mirage could be advantageous for morale this late in the game. Their eyes focused on the tiny speck in the distance. Without even thinking about it, they had their hand in the water trying to help speed up the group's arrival.

In time, even Harper saw the smidgen of land off in the distance. "Holy crap. Azi! You were right!"

Azi grimaced, "You don't have to sound so surprised."

He didn't paddle when he spoke, and it took everything Moxxi had not to snatch the makeshift oar from his hand and put it back to use.

Harper must have had similar thoughts, because she didn't even talk back to her five-year-old counterpart. She just agreed silently, and waited for him to keep going.

That was the theme of this journey: waiting on

Azi for everything. Moxxi had no idea how someone could get so distracted with absolutely no new stimulus around them, but he excelled at it. He'd row ten, fifteen, possibly even twenty times. Then, he'd pause. Sometimes he'd sit down, sometimes he'd stick his feet or hands in the water to play, sometimes he even tried to fully lay down and stretch out over Harper. Moxxi anticipated he would be a slower navigator than the two older options, but they did not anticipate for him to need a thousand breaks when land was finally in sight. LAND! Which, evidently, did not matter. Azi was very much of the "we'll get there when we get there" variety.

After what Moxxi considered to be an excruciatingly long amount of time, they could finally start to distinguish parts of their destination. This was no ordinary island. This was a jungle. Trees were lush, tall, and bountiful. Vines wove around the base like their sole responsibility was to contain the land's size within its grasp. The spaces in-between the trees were dark and ominous. The smell was potent of fresh soil and vegetation. It was picturesque and mildly menacing.

Harper had noticed a beach off to the left side of the island and convinced Azi to steer their watercraft that way to avoid having to scale large boulders with potentially poisonous plants. It was a rather straightforward decision to be made, but only if a person felt like being practical which, to no surprise of Moxxi, the very tired child did not. Azi protested any decision that was not his to begin with.

He sat the paddle down again. “I don’t feel appreciated!” He exclaimed.

Oh my gosh. I might start screaming. Pick up the paddle for the love of your preferred pantheon!

“I found the ANIMALS. I found the ISLAND. I should hear NOTHING but praise from BOTH of you, but do I? NO. You don’t even believe me when I tell you things. You’re such HATERS!”

Harper took a deep breath before restating her position. “All I said, Azi, was that maybe scaling jagged, pointy rocks wrapped in unknown vines should not be our first choice when there is a perfectly sandy beach within sight.” Her words started a rapid-fire argument with the small boy.

“You can only see a chunk of it! You don’t know what’s there!”

“We don’t know what the things we can’t see are either!”

“We would know if they were in front of our face!”

“Even if they were in front of our face, and we decided they weren’t trying to kill us, we would still have to find a way up a wall that’s taller than the last house we saw.”

“YOU’RE the one always bragging about your skills and your endurance! You a chicken now?”

“I’m not a chicken. I’m just not—” Harper caught her tongue before her anger said words she couldn’t take back. “—I just see no sense in choosing the harder path when there's an easier one not that far off."

Azi stood, bent his arms to make chicken wings, and started clucking at Harper, hopping from foot to foot and rocking the couch from side to side.

Moxxi watched as Harper's mouth kept opening and closing, no doubt trying to pick her words carefully. They wanted to help her out. Interacting with five-year-olds was way more taxing than it looked sometimes. "Azi!"

He ignored the warning and continued with more squawking, more flapping, and more water soaking their seating area.

Harper screamed at the ocean before facing the small boy. "THAT IS IT! I HAVE HAD IT FROM YOU AZARIAH COCA! YOU SIT DOWN THIS INSTANT!"

He leaned forward and sneered in Harper's face. "You can't make me! You're not the boss of me!"

Harper reached out for the unoccupied paddle. "I am done. You are tired, and you need a nap. I'm taking over."

"YOU WILL NOT!" And that's when Azi leapt from his cushion and tackled Harper into the sea.

Their scuffle would have been humorous if Moxxi had not desperately wanted to move forward with or without them. Shouts of "Go to bed" and "I'm not tired" were continuous and muffled by heads being dunked under the water. Ripples moved the couch further and further away. Moxxi used the paddle to keep the sofa from going too far off track. The distance was growing uncomfortable when Moxxi caught a better glimpse of the beach.

There was something written in the sand. Moxxi read the note inscribed on the shore, "*Get out! Not yours!*", with a small drawing at the end. "Umm, Azi." The kerfuffle was still going strong. Moxxi slapped the paddle on the water making a painful splashing sound. "AZI!"

Harper held him above the water. He fought until he realized it wasn't part of their battle.

Moxxi hastily waved them over. "Come here, please. Quickly. You need to see this."

The two obliged without hesitation. Harper swam a perfect breaststroke over to the couch, and Azi held on to her shoulders as she did so.

"There." Moxxi pointed to the picture in the sand. It was not the best drawing they had ever seen, but it had a circle for a head, a few smaller circles for eyes, a heart for a nose, a curly shape for a mouth, and two long droopy ears on the side. It was a bunny. Which meant, it was likely to be Brownie.

Azi spoke tearfully, "Amari."

Harper swore under her breath.

"We have to go, Harps! We have to go NOW! We have to go get my sister!!!"

Paddle already in hand, Harper was crouched and eager. "On it!"

Moxxi did what they could from behind with

their hands.

"AMARI!" Azi beckoned. "AMARI I'M HERE!"

Moxxi kept an eye on the boy. His demeanor had flipped 180 degrees from before, and now, they were unsure if he would dive off the edge and start swimming out of impatience.

A rustling in the leaves behind the trees stole Moxxi's focus. *Of course, something knows we're here; we've lacked all discreteness.* A small girl, about Azi's size, broke through the jungle's dense barrier. Her mouth was gaping open in astonishment and in her arms, was a giant floppy brown rabbit plushie.

That's her. That's the girl from the hospital. Moxxi expected this to be true, but the surprise of seeing her again hit hard nonetheless. *She's real.*

The faux boat bumped the sandy coastline about a hundred yards away from Amari. Harper jumped into the water, scooped Azi onto her back without any form of communication, and got him to the beach with haste. Moxxi jumped in behind them, but without knowing how to swim, their journey was much slower and significantly less efficient.

By the time Moxxi made their way to the second small child, another person was present on the outskirts of the foliage. She was smaller than Harper, but even at a distance, Moxxi could tell she was bigger than the twins. They assumed this figure had to be Gwen, especially with how frantically Harper was doting over her, and that her age was around twelve years old. Her skin was half-light and half-dark in an irregular blotchy pattern, and her head was slightly misshapen. Moxxi couldn't quite figure out the words they wanted to understand Gwen's appearance. The best word they could come up with at the moment was: blurry.

"HARPS! HARPS! Come here please!" Azi demanded in an exasperated tone. "You need to talk some sense into this immature child, PLEASE!" He sneered at his sister as he spoke.

Moxxi got to the young duo first.

Amari was not having it. "Azi! You never listen, you tattle tale! She told me you would come, but I didn't want to believe it. You shouldn't be here! I'm so glad you're here, but you need to leave!"

Moxxi didn't expect to hear that. *Who told Amari we were coming? Gwen?*

"I'm here to SAVE you! Get that through your thick skull!" He tapped his sister's head.

"Don't touch me! I didn't give you permission to do that, you big bully! HARPER!"

"All right. All right. Calm down, you two." Harper stepped in the middle of the kids, Gwen trailing behind her.

Moxxi offered a smile and waved to the mysterious tween.

Gwen's eyes were kind and warm when she reciprocated the greeting.

Harper, on the other hand, noticed nothing on account of having her hands full with the twins. "What is going on?"

Both five-year-olds started yelling at once.

"My fault!" Harper raised her hands to the air in defeat. "My fault. Amari first."

Azi kicked sand and grumbled under his breath how Amari always gets to go first.

The little girl coughed and glared at her brother before she started her explanation. "Like I was TRYING to tell HIM, I'm really glad to see you, but you need to go."

"To go? You want us to leave?" Harper confirmed.

"Yes. This is my private island." She pointed to the words on the shore. "No one is supposed to be able to come here but me, and if YOU can get here, then so can that icky eyeball, and I just—" Rumbling on the ground cut off her words. "NO!" She shrieked. "IT'S NOT SUPPOSED TO HAPPEN LIKE THIS! Everyone! RUN! Follow me!" And Amari darted into the dark dense tree-line. Gwen grabbed Harper who grabbed Azi, and they ran linked together doing their best to catch up to Amari.

Moxxi started to run, but something pulled at them to stop. They wanted to look back. They wanted to turn around. Amari's pleas suddenly felt disjointed and barely made any sense in their memory. Maybe Amari didn't know as much as she claimed, and Moxxi could find actual truths. They were compelled to return to the water. An overwhelming urge pulled at them to separate from the rest of their pack.

A glitchy voice entered their mind. It sounded

like blaring radio static, but between the harsh noises a few words were audible. "Come to me. Leave them behind."

Moxxi stopped their half-hearted sprint and stared towards the sky. That's when they saw it. They watched El Ojo, clear as day, descend from the clouds above. An enormous red-skinned eyeball with a sloshy crimson iris lowered itself to the ground with the pumping of its four barbed, moldy, tentacles trailing behind it.

Moxxi opened their mouth to speak, but a firm fist on the collar of their shirt broke their line of thought.

"You are the absolute worst human being I have ever met, and if I die for this, I will never forgive you. Do you understand that? Can you use your legs please? Are you trying to make this as hard as you physically can?" Harper chastised passionately. "Seriously? Do you have a death wish? Should I just drop you here? USE YOUR LEGS!!!!"

Moxxi's brain finally caught up. They did as they were told, and off they ran into the jungle out of sight from that awful, horrid, ocular abomination. The ground vibrated below their feet. "That thing is disgusting!"

"I wouldn't know. I didn't stay long enough to shake its hand. What were you thinking?" Harper criticized from ahead.

What was I thinking? I was thinking . . . I was thinking I needed to get closer to them and ditch my friends. "There's a chance it was messing with my head?"

Harper scoffed. "Convenient excuse, Moxxi."

"I'm serious! I heard it talk to me!" Moxxi proclaimed.

"You what? I can't believe you'd be that naive! Since when is it a good idea to let evil eyeballs into your mind, Moxxi?"

"You don't really get a choice." Gwen added sullenly.

Harper's tone pivoted on a dime. "I bet. I'm sorry that happened to you, Gwen."

You've got to be kidding me. Moxxi couldn't believe that Gwen received so much grace for the same thing they were being raked over the coals for.

"In here!" Amari shouted and held open a curtain of moss and leaves that revealed a small safehouse.

Azi was the first to enter, then Gwen. Harper ushered Moxxi in next and followed behind. Amari sealed the entrance closed as the last one in.

"We should be okay here. La Madre should protect us."

"La Madre?" Moxxi asked. They translated the meaning quickly. "Your mother?"

Azi was quick to answer. "Our mother is dead."

He stated it so factually that Moxxi wasn't sure how to respond. *Why is he not sad over that?*

Amari continued, "She protects me here. She's who built this island for me and told me you would come and kept my safe space safe."

"Have you been here the whole time?" Harper wanted to know.

"Yup yup! At least, most of it. El Ojo captured me that day that I lost Azi, but by the time he gave me Brownie back, I was already spending most of my time here." Amari kissed the top of her plushie's head. "El Ojo was never able to find me here . . . until today." She glared at her brother.

"That's not my fault! Don't be blaming me! How about you say THANK YOU for getting your bunny back!" Azi waited for praise that had no intention of existing. "Well, you're WELCOME." He embellished the last part with jazz hands.

"It could be my fault," Gwen suggested. "You said it yourself that things haven't been acting right lately, which in Amari terms means since I got here. First it was that dead flower, then that dead patch of vines, and then . . . then that other dead thing." Gwen cringed. "I'm sorry. I didn't mean to bring that up again."

Amari was sitting on the ground, with her knees up to her chin, clutching Brownie with her childish fists.

Harper, wanting to distract, kept talking. "The reason doesn't matter. El Ojo is here now, and we need to defeat it."

"Can we do that?" Moxxi questioned under their breath.

"No," Azi replied flatly. "You can't win against

anything here. Why would the super eyeball be any different?"

"Everything has a weakness." Harper attempted to convince him.

He didn't want to hear it and waved her off.

Moxxi struggled. They didn't think either of the two was wrong. Wisps tickled their fingers. They saw Gwen standing near them. A thought overcame their mind. *Day of Judgement is near.* "Oh." The word escaped their mouth.

"Everything okay?" Gwen checked-in compassionately.

Not for you, but I can't tell you that here. "My mind is just a little off. No big deal."

Gwen was sympathetic. She grabbed Moxxi's hand. "I feel off more often than not lately."

Moxxi knew why. Gwen was dying. Her soul was almost ready for transport, but they couldn't tell her that, not yet, not now, not in The Backrooms. That would be a conversation for future Moxxi to handle out in the real world.

Overhearing Gwen's comment, Harper chimed in. "I packed your drinks! Want one?" She dug in her bag and pulled out an almond water.

Gwen took it happily.

"Since we can't beat him, we need to get back to camp and keep trying to figure out a way to go home." Azi was clear in his announcement.

"I don't think it's that easy," Gwen countered.

"And I can't leave." Amari sobbed. "I'm never

going to go home again!" Tears chased her words.

A crackle of thunder boomed overhead.

"Amari! No! Don't cry!" Azi shouted at the ceiling.

Her wails filled the room. Rain began to pour hard, and water rapidly began to rise inside their safe space.

Part IX

The water was climbing up to Moxxi's knees, and a current was pulling them off their feet. Harper had already picked up Azi and put him on her back for the third time. Gwen was crowding them, making sure the duo didn't lose balance. Amari was an immovable object.

"I TOLD YOU! Didn't I?" Azi shouted. "I told you she gets like this!"

"Yes, yes, all right. You win. You told us everything and were right the whole time. But what I need to know now is how do we get her to stop?" Harper pandered.

"You don't. You just have to ride out her storm." Lightning crackled through the safe house as Azi spoke, igniting the ceiling on fire.

Moxxi jumped away from the flames trailing down the walls and joined the others. "We can't stay here."

"There's nowhere to go," Gwen replied. "We either burn in here or face El Ojo."

Moxxi nodded. "That's exactly my point. We need to leave this hideout."

"Do you even have a plan?" Harper probed.

Moxxi's only thoughts were to persuade everyone to stop talking and get out of this burning house. "Of course! We just need some space to make it all work." *And less fire, less flooding, and less crying would be nice too.*

Harper splashed some water on herself and Gwen, threw a wet blanket floating at her feet over Azi, and made her way out into the jungle. That left Moxxi to figure out how to move Amari.

They got down on one knee in front of the small girl. They were not used to children, but they had seen more than one adult throw a tantrum during their duties. Moxxi had never tried to calm the upset adults, they believed grown-ups should be mature enough to handle their own emotional regulation, but that excuse wouldn't clear Moxxi's moral compass with a five-year-old. There was no avoiding this situation. Moxxi tried to think of what would have calmed them at that age, but Moxxi wasn't entirely sure they ever were that age.

The branch directly above Amari had been lit ablaze and was crackling and popping. Out of the corner of their eye, Moxxi saw it start to droop. They threw themselves over Amari and Brownie as the blazing plant fell onto them. "Ahh!" The pain was brutal, they knew it would scar their back, but Moxxi didn't move. They kept themselves firmly positioned above the small child. *Columbia. MadreMonte. Return to the land.*

Amari gasped. The rains, thunder, and lightning halted abruptly. “Oh no! That’s not supposed to hurt YOU! You should’ve let it fall!”

Moxxi’s agony made it hard to talk. “And . . . let it . . . hurt . . . you . . . instead? Not an . . . option.”

“You don’t understand! It wouldn’t have hurt me! It would have just fallen into the water!” Amari was so sure of herself.

Moxxi gestured to her plushie. “Brow . . . nie.”

“Oh. I don’t know if MadreMonte protects Brownie, but she probably does? Right? He’s never gotten hurt so far.” The small child was utterly neutral in her deliberation. Her raging emotions had completely stabilized.

You flooded out your house and then lit it on fire. How does that not phase you? Moxxi squinted at the girl.

Amari looked around. “Where did everyone go?” She went to a nearby wall and pulled out a scorched plastic case. “I can fix you. Come here.”

Moxxi was ushered onto a chair partially submerged in the water, then a chilled goopy liquid was squirted onto their back over their shirt and burn marks. “That’s cold!” They shouted in shock.

“You're healed. Can we go to the others now?”

And I thought your brother was a handful. “Sure.” Moxxi let Amari out the door first, not even bothering to check their wounds.

"I was just about to go back in for you two!" Harper declared.

"Uh, thanks. I think we're fine?" Moxxi wanted to talk in detail about how uncanny they thought Amari was, but couldn't figure out how to do it with their eyes.

An ear-piercing screech sounded from above.

"We knew it was only a matter of time," Gwen acknowledged.

Amari stomped her feet, and the jungle's canopy grew visibly denser. "You're not supposed to be here! This is my island! It was made for ME! GO AWAY!"

"Amari, you said MadreMonte built this for you. Is she here? Can she help? What else can she do?" Moxxi was anxious for some easy answers.

"Umm. I don't really know. I saw her once though! She was beautiful and so big!! I really liked her hat."

That was not the answer Moxxi wanted or needed.

Another bone rattling screech then a cacophony of snaps began growing in speed towards them. Everyone turned in rapt attention. El Ojo was propelling itself through the trees, its pupil at front and center, opening into a small maw with needle-like teeth as it shrieked at its escapees.

"Run!" Harper screamed, dragging the twins with her. Gwen pushed the kid's backs to help them move faster.

Moxxi ran as fast as they could, but if the others were already struggling to stay ahead, they stood no chance in outrunning the disgusting eyeball. Their body was not made for this. *Harper has been right all along; I can't keep up with everyone. I will always lag behind. So, if that's the way it is, then that's the way it shall be.* Accepting their fate, they knew what they needed to do next. Their best way to contribute was to be bait and buy the others time. Moxxi let themself trip over a tree root and shook their hands fervently. *Shadow form? No. Torch? Still no. Shadow form? Come on!!! Torch?*

El Ojo moved at an inhuman speed towards its prey.

Work! Give me something! Anything! Shadow? Torch? Stick? Stick! It wasn't a superpower, but they had found a hardy tree limb on the ground next to them.

As El Ojo neared, it rose into the air, tentacles flailing in the sky, and prepped itself to plunge onto its target.

Moxxi reassured themself in what they knew would be their final moments. *Don't be afraid. If there's one thing we know, it's death.* Stick in hand, they were ready to meet their end.

The pupil opened wide, extending its jaw farther and farther until it was wide enough to devour a human, and so it did. Moxxi had been eaten. The stick they attempted to use to jam the mouth open, was broken in half immediately. It stood no chance and neither did the disciple of Mors. *Mors.*

The inside was black and tarry and gooey and sticky. “This is sickening.” They chided. Moxxi rose to their feet and attempted to walk around. At best, they hoped to find the command center of the eye. They wanted to ensure that everyone else was okay and if they could, potentially steer the creature elsewhere. At worst, they thought maybe they could find those who met a similar fate and learn something useful about El Ojo.

Mors. His name played over and over in Moxxi’s mind. In some ways, if they were going to have their own afterlife, they were happy it was in a place he couldn’t reach them. They had never seen the god of death do his dirty work, but they didn’t get the vibe he was the nicest of guys.

Mors. Nox. Nox? That name was unexpected. They had never delivered someone to Nox before. Nox was the Roman goddess of night, and Mors’ parent figure. *Wasn’t Nox a primordial goddess?* Primordial deities were not to be messed with. Anything that had been around since the birth of existence likely amassed magic that could be catastrophic to the world as a whole. That balance had to be tipped as minimally as possible.

If I die, do I go to Nox instead of Mors? Does being born of Mors mean I need to go somewhere else? The longer they stayed in this pitch-black prison, the more they wondered if they were no longer with El Ojo after all. *Nox. Scotus. Scotus?* That name was even more foreign than Nox. "Scotus . . . Scotus . . . what is a Scotus?" Moxxi wondered aloud, trying to jog something within their memory.

A familiar screech vibrated so strongly around Moxxi's head they wondered if their ear drums would rupture at the noise. "Who dares to call upon the child of Chaos in my presence? Am I not enough for you? Dare I make it worse?"

Moxxi's eyes remained blinded, but the sneer and cheshire smile of that last sentence was prominently conveyed. *Scotus is the child of Chaos. Why does El Ojo care about Scotus?* A soft glow appeared around their neck. Reflexively, they fiddled with their necklace Fukurokuju had given them. The light was warm to their touch, it felt comforting, it felt like being home. A memory clicked into place. "That's right. Child of Chaos, God of Darkness, Second Ruler of the Cosmos."

"You know nothing!" The voice jeered.

A heavy smack came to the side of the room, and Moxxi was thrown against the side of the cell. *Mors. Nox.* Another shriek resounded. It didn't appear to be inflicted from anything Moxxi had done. *The others found an advantage. They're fighting back.*

A voice overtook the room again. Not a sharp spiked voice like El Ojo, a deep voice. A calm, steady, flowing voice. "Your presence is not welcomed on this land. You are a mischief-maker."

Again and again, the room battered into an unseen object, and Moxxi was flung backwards and forwards and backwards and forwards. They were getting dizzy. They felt a splintering headache forming in the back of their mind.

"I'm going to puke inside of you. Is that really what you want?"

Revolted, El Ojo threatened. "How dare you defile me, human! I will end you if I must!"

"I'm not human." Moxxi shook their hand out of habit, and much to their amazement, an ornate golden torch appeared within their grasp.

The eye hissed and spun. "The torch of Mors! That's impossible!"

"I assure you it is not." Relief spread like wildfire within Moxxi. *I've missed you, old friend.*

"In order to summon that, you would have to be a child of Mors!"

"I am, and after you perish, it'll be me who takes you to your end." Moxxi bent down and dug their hand into the grotesque muck of El Ojo. *Nox.* Moxxi was stupefied. "When your time comes, you are to be delivered to Nox . . ."

"You have no say over me! I am immortal! Get out of me, foul child, banished are thee!"

Moxxi braced themself as an opening with a needle-filled rim formed before them. "If you are to be returned to Nox, that means—" They didn't even get to finish their thought before they were hurled towards the trees below.

"You're not getting away that easy." Moxxi was set in their pursuit. They shook their hands, and turned into a torch-lit shadow bolting upwards back into the sky. “Nox.” El Ojo’s voice tried to scream once again, but Moxxi was undeterred. “Mother of Mors.” The eye hissed and spit as Moxxi rose above it. “Mother of Discordia.” A growl that shook the entire world was emitted from Moxxi’s foe. “She will reclaim her children when their time comes, and she will ensure their time will come so they never outpower their own mother.”

El Ojo, or rather Discordia, lunged to attack the shadow hovering over them. Moxxi dodged, and with their arm raised high, they plunged the torch into the goddess’ manifestation. “By the power of Mors, you, Discordia, have overstepped your Roman limits, you have over asserted your Roman powers, and now you must be returned to your mother and be punished for your crimes by the child of Chaos, Second Ruler of the Cosmos, the Primordial God, Scotus. Mors will deliver you to your final judgement. Your brother awaits your return.” Feeling the anger, frustrations, and fears of their entire time here, Moxxi plummeted the torch deep within their opponent until there was no more resistance, and Discordia had been vanquished for good.

The banishment had the force of the gods behind it. It had sent Moxxi catapulting to the ground. As a shadow, they barely made a thud as they hit a rather lush patch of grass that had not been there seconds earlier. They could hear Azi’s voice. “I knew they weren’t useless! Go Moxxi! Woohoo!” He applauded, running up to them, and wrapping their legs in a big hug.

Moxxi was unsure of his arrival. "You guys shouldn't be here. What if that ugly eyeball survived?"

"Five minutes with my brother, and they'd poof all on their own." Amari oozed condescension.

Harper sighed, raising her arms in defeat. "I can barely handle one Coca twin when they're set in their ways. I stood no chance with the two of them."

"Yup! That's right!" Azi fist bumped his sister, who begrudgingly participated.

Gwen stepped into view. "How did you know you could do that?"

I didn't. "It just happened. I spent enough time with them that I just knew what came next." *This realm rivaled Jupiter's and there was no way his pantheon would allow a minor goddess to have supremacy like this.* The ground shook beneath Moxxi's feet. Chunks of The Backrooms were plummeting to the ground. They crashed into each other and left gaping wounds in the fabric of this reality. *This realm! Discordia's realm! It can't exist without her. I dismantled this entire world! Crap!*

Moxxi avoided collisions with a shark tank, a suburban two-story house, a block of a full moon, and a cubic field of wheat. Arms reached out from the fragments that fell, grasping for anything or anyone to hold onto. This domain was literally crumbling around them, and Moxxi needed to find a way to get their friends out of this mess.

Moxxi knew what they had to do. They morphed into their soul transporter mode, donned their traditional garb, all while trying to reassure their friends. “I’ve got you!” Moxxi swept up the twins, Harper, and Gwen and carried their souls as far away from the imploding world as they could.

With their trusty torch still in hand, they thrust it in front of them and let it navigate a path back to the real world.

Part X

The pathway back home twisted all over. There was no way a single person could have handled this without proper assistance. Moxxi was grateful to feel whole again and have all their skills readily available. The best part, by far, was being able to travel without worry. Despite its complexity, the void between worlds was serene. Nothing and everything existed together in perfect harmony. As long as you knew how to get to your destination, it was smooth sailing. Not to mention that souls, as far as Moxxi understood it, weren't able to talk during transport, which meant the whole trip was rather tranquil. There was something comforting about life feeling like it had returned to normal. They doubted that it would last once they landed back in the hospital.

Moxxi could have taken the quartet anywhere, they supposed. However, they hadn't asked any questions before sweeping their friends out of harm's way and transforming the group into a cluster of souls. They were a little nervous about how everyone was going to react to that, but Moxxi had panicked. If they could have had a proper conversation, maybe the destination would be less of a downer but also, maybe the weight of the world would have fallen on top of everyone, and all five of them would have been crushed under a pile of their former reality's fallen rubble. Who was to say? Not Moxxi.

They could feel the energy of the living world drawing near. "I don't know if you can hear me, but we're closing in on the world you came from. You'll be home in three . . . two . . . one." Moxxi shielded their travelers as they went through a wall into what they hoped would be a vacant hospital room. Moxxi released their guests.

All four of them rubbed their heads. Harper found a chair to sit in, while the twins stayed on the floor. Gwen was the only one with their wits about them.

"I haven't been here in a long, long time." Gwen's voice was rougher here. Their shape was both more and less distinct. Their image of what they looked like was crisper, but their overall form looked much closer to a soul, an essence of their being, more than it did a physical form.

They don't belong on this plane. They're going to need to travel with me again to go to their final resting place sooner than later. Moxxi understood the reality, even if they didn't want to force the issue just yet.

"What was that, Moxxi? That was trippier than

anything I've been through in years." Harper complained.

"Sorry about that. The good news is that I think I banished Discordia successfully for the time being, at least until her pantheon deals with her, but the bad news was that it made the entire realm we were living in crumble to pieces. I freaked out and did the one thing I knew how to do under any circumstance."

"You transported us?" Azi verified.

Moxxi nodded. "I did."

Amari had a funny expression on her face. "What does that mean?"

"It means you're home. Or at least at the location where your dream was based on when we first met."

Azi looked around, his eyes wide. "You took us to where our mom died?"

Moxxi's jaw dropped. They had no idea that's why Amari lingered around here.

"It's not a bad thing," Amari comforted. "Mom wouldn't have fully passed on while we were lost in that ugly place. Let's go find her, Azi, and tell her we're back home! No more creepy yellow hallways for us!"

Moxxi tried to interject, but Azi's agreement muffled out any protests, and the two walked straight past the security doors outside the room without anyone giving them a blink of an eye. Moxxi looked to Harper and Gwen for backup and found none. "That's going to be a problem, isn't it?" They asked, referring to the small children who were now roaming free in a medical facility. "Shouldn't we go do something? Stop them? Keep them contained?"

"Have you met the twins?" Gwen chided. "They're home now. Let them find their mom."

Harper concurred. "I'm with Gwen on this one. It's been a while since we've all been here."

"How long?" Moxxi tried to downplay their curiosity.

"2001 for me." Harper found the date on the dry erase board near her. "Over twenty years ago, it seems."

Gwen was scoping out the room too. "I'm about twenty behind you. It was still 1980 when I got attacked and they brought me here."

Over forty years in total. That's a long time for a human life. "What—" Moxxi wasn't sure how to ask what they wanted without sounding insensitive "—how—"

"How did we end up here?" Harper offered.

Gwen laughed. "You don't know?"

"I don't . . ." Moxxi was deeply tongue-tied.

"I was in a coma when I got sucked into The Backrooms. Something was wrong with my blood sugars. I didn't really understand what that meant and never had the time to figure it out before things got bad. I watched myself sleep and my family cry. A voice offered to help, so I followed it into a black abyss. You know the rest from there." Harper took a moment to process her words. “Wow. Twenty years almost. I can’t believe it lasted so long.”

Emotions were rising within Gwen. “I was in worse shape. I remember hearing the beep of my pulse on the machine, but that’s it. I was in dire straits after that guy used his Glock on me. I tried to just give him the money we had in the house, but it wasn’t enough.” Tears were trickling down her cheek.

“I feel awful. I had no idea.” Moxxi was ashamed of their mistake.

“Don’t be.” Harper put her hand on Moxxi’s shoulder. “We all needed closure.”

A new question was forming in Moxxi’s mind. “What about the kids?”

“I’ve never been totally sure.” Harper admitted. “Do you know, Gwen?”

“I feel like Amari mentioned they were left on life support after the accident?” She suggested.

“Yeah. That makes sense with the bits and pieces Azi has alluded to. They were much more recent though, if I remember correctly?” It had been a while since Azi had talked about his former life to Harper.

Gwen nodded. “That makes sense to me. They definitely don’t talk like kids in the 80’s did, and I doubt the decades before me used the word ‘noob.’”

Harper laughed. “Azi absolutely has a way with words. There’s no denying that.”

“There were some mentions of gadgets too that made me think they were from a more advanced time. I intentionally avoided learning more. I didn't want to know."

"That's right." Harper recalled. "They used to ask for our smart phones when they first joined us. It sounded so different from what I grew up with. I think you're spot on."

Gwen was proud of her contributions. "But, Moxxi, I'm surprised. I figured you'd have known this all already."

Moxxi found no need to lie this far into the conversation. "I'm not privy to anything the gods don't want me to know. Mors tries to keep it to the moment's information only. I can stretch those boundaries a bit, but usually, I'm just told things in real time." Moxxi simplified the process the best they could.

Gwen's voice turned solemn. "Did you hear anything about me?"

"I have."

Gwen was satisfied with the answer. "That seems right to me." She paused, taking the room in. "I don't think I belong here, Moxxi."

They were straight forward in their delivery. "You don't, not for your final stop."

"Will you take me to whatever that final stop is after this?"

"I can. Whenever you're ready." Moxxi was not one to offer extra time, but this was a unique situation.

"What happens to the rest of us then?" Harper's tone came off desperate. "I don't even know where my body is."

In all the times Moxxi had been close to Harper, no names had been dropped into Moxxi's mind. They had no information on Harper at all, and Moxxi decided that was the best outcome. "I don't think it's your time yet. I think you're still supposed to live, Harper."

"Like this? That's not even an option!"

She had a point; Moxxi couldn't deny that. "How about the three of us take a walk then? It'll be a good excuse to find the twins anyway. Fully human or not, they can get into a lot of trouble in a very small amount of time."

Relieved, Harper obliged. "And you have no idea how much of a handful they can be together."

It didn't take long to find the little ones. Their voices tended to fill any space they were in. Moxxi spotted Amari first.

"You should have seen it! Mountains shot into the sky like bullets, and it trapped the icky eyeball, and it bounced around like a pinball, and it got so tired, and . . . and . . . and it was so cool!"

Moxxi spied on them before entering the room. A small lump lay curled in the bed in front of the little girl.

"I helped too! If it wasn't for Ebisu, I don't think anyone would've found you. Harper and Moxxi were lost without me. I was like their hero or something. Everything I said and did, they were BLOWN AWAY about how AWESOME and SMART I was. You should ask them sometime. I'm sure they'd tell you. They can't stop talking about me like EVER."

Moxxi had to cover their mouth to not diminish his moment. They came around the corner, lightly rapping on the door. "Knock, knock."

Azi's face swiftly reddened. Moxxi was going to reassure him, but the wispy outline of a tall, slender, adult woman beat them to it.

"You must be one of their friends. How lovely. They simply can't stop talking about you." She gave a knowing wink. "I'm Jade Coca, their mother."

Moxxi bowed their head. "It's a pleasure, ma'am."

"I can certainly tell. It's been fifty long weeks watching over them, but from the sounds of it, this may have been the easier side of things." She smiled sweetly.

Moxxi knew that wasn't true. Feeling helpless was so much worse than fighting and running. "They're good kids. Reuniting their family was always their first priority."

Jade blinked slowly and wiped the corner of her eye. "They're my everything."

Moxxi knew that to be true, even before stepping into this room.

"Mama?" Amari called out.

"Yes, sweetheart?"

"What happens now? My body looks so lumpy."

"I'm . . . I'm not sure. I imagine, somehow, you'll go back and wake up, now that you're home. It could take some time though. I don't know much about things like this, I'm afraid."

Moxxi assumed they knew how to rejoin a soul to a body, but it'd mean losing the ability to see their mom. They knew they would be the one to help them along in this situation. Eventually.

Azi tapped on his unconscious face. "Wake up! You're missing out on all the cool things you didn't know you were up to!"

Jade stepped closer to Moxxi and spoke so her children couldn't hear. "This is all I get, isn't it?"

Moxxi wasn't sure how to answer that in an uplifting way.

"I am so glad to see them back, but that means our time is coming to an end, I bet."

Amari overheard and came over to hold onto her mother's hand. "You can't leave, Mama!" Tears were welling in her eyes.

"Shhhhhhh." Jade wiped away the tears with her thumbs, held her daughter's face, and kissed her forehead. "This is the way it was supposed to be."

"No!" Azi, catching on, protested.

"Once my energy is returned to the Earth, I will be everywhere you are. We'll find each other again. I'm sure of it." Jade held her twins close.

Moxxi looked away. This wasn't their moment to partake in, and they couldn't make the same promises to the family that were currently being said.

"Who is going to take care of us?" Amari sniffled into her mother's chest.

Fear flashed on Jade's face. "That is an excellent question. I think I need to have an adult conversation for that."

"I'm an adult now! Didn't you hear all the cool things I did?" Azi was getting riled up at his mother's implications. "Moxxi, tell her how I'm the BEST! Tell her how I did ALL the things and how grateful you all were for ME!"

"Now, now. Settle down, Azariah. I think you have some other friends here, yes? I would like to meet them while I can. Why don't you two wait outside, and behave like my good little five-year-olds, while I have a moment with Moxxi. I'll be right there, and then we can find this Harper and Gwen you speak of. Understood?"

The twins grumped in unison. "Understood."

Jade escorted them out and shut the door behind them. "I am sure you can sense my concern."

Moxxi acknowledged her statement but didn't speak.

"You're basically still a child yourself, so I am not asking you to take care of my precious babies. However, since I imagine I'll lose my presence in this world soon, I need to beseech a favor from you."

Moxxi continued to nod but not speak.

"Their father, Mateo, is a very dangerous man. Dangerous enough to cause the accident that landed us in the predicament we're in. He's going to want the children. They're . . . special, and he knows that. He will do everything he can to obtain possession of them if he finds out they're alive and healthy. He'll use their abilities to enhance his current market in the Columbian trades. I won't ask you to promise the impossible, but can you please say you'll try to put them with someone or place them somewhere that protects their wellbeing? I would do it myself, but—but it's probably preferable to request aid at this point of time."

Moxxi should've been shocked at this, but somewhere in their mind, they suspected the kids might need a guardian, and that guardian couldn't be of the ordinary variety. "I don't know if it'll work, but I do have one thought in mind."

Jade's face lit up like Azi's so frequently did. Her kids had all of her best qualities. "Truly?"

"I have a single idea on who I can ask, but yes, I have a place in mind."

Jade wrapped her arms around Moxxi, and they could feel a weight being lifted from Jade's spirit. She pulled away shortly after, embarrassment creeping in now that her mind was back on track. "Oh my. What an outburst. I apologize for that. I don't know what came over me."

I do. It was hope. Moxxi had not seen much hope in the human souls they transported, but lately they were starting to understand just how powerful it could be to the human spirit.

"Thank you for taking my concerns seriously. I

trust you'll keep my twins as safe as you can. I know firsthand how much that is asking of you, but there is nothing more important to me than their safety." Jade's words were heavy and earnest. "I believe it will be the difference between being at rest and being restless."

"No soul should spend eternity on edge. I'm happy to do what I can in the best way I can."

"You're very formal, Moxxi. I like that about you. Are the others as proper as you are?"

They've lived their own lives; they're so superior to me. "Their hearts far exceed my own."

Jade smirked. "I'll be the judge of that. Go ahead and take me to them."

Moxxi did as instructed. Jade rounded up her children. Moxxi found Harper and Gwen who had, in turn, found Harper's body exactly where she had left it.

"It's weird, right? Staring at yourself?" She poked her aged self continuously.

The room smelled fresh in here. It was bright and colorful and had an unexpected surprise. "Harper, are those fresh flowers?"

"Huh? Oh, yeah. My sister brought them up with my mom when they were here."

Your sister and your mom were here?

"That's how we found the room." Gwen disclosed.

Harper continued. "I saw them in the hallway, and we crept behind them. I don't know why. They can't see us, but I didn't want to spook them. They're old now. Old people spook easier than us kids." She then took notice of Ms. Coca. "No offense to you."

"None taken." Jade waived her hand in the air in a graceful fashion.

Moxxi could see how flawless Ms. Coca would have presented herself to be when she was alive; she emitted elegance even in death.

"I don't mean to rush you, but my senses are tingling." Moxxi joked. The room didn't quite catch on that they weren't being literal. "It's about that time."

Azi tugged on Harper's backpack. "Will you still remember me when you wake up?"

She ruffled his hair. "Azi, I don't think I will ever be able to forget you. Come find me when you feel up for it. I'll be waiting for you."

"Me too!" Amari added, wrapped tight around her mother.

"You three?" Harper proposed to Gwen.

"I don't think it works like that, my friend."

"But if it does?"

Gwen smiled a mischievous smile. "If it does, I will haunt you so bad there will be no mistaking it's me."

That broke Harper. She hugged Gwen before the rest of the room could see her tears. "You better! I'm going to be so mad if you're just moping around wasting all that potential. You find me, and you haunt me until I can yell at you again. You got that?"

Gwen smoothed Harper's hair. "I didn't expect

it to end this way either. I wouldn't have left if it were anyone else."

Harper's words were barely audible. "I know, I know. This is what we wanted anyway. It just still sucks."

"It does."

Moxxi had witnessed thousands of final moments, but none were ever like this. The souls they transported were never together with their loved ones. Most were lost and wandering about, rarely even from the current time period. In Moxxi's worst situations, the souls were stolen and improperly placed back into the world. By the time Moxxi came around to them, most of them tended to be rather dull and resigned. Moxxi couldn't decide if that was their preferred option over this level of emotion. These goodbyes hurt. That wasn't how Moxxi thought goodbyes should feel.

"All right. How do we do this?" Harper had let go of Gwen and was back by her comatose body.

Moxxi had never done this before, but it seemed simple enough. It was still a transport, just in a slightly different direction. "Hold the hands of your body, and I'll touch both your shoulders." This part was probably performative, but every now and then, dramatics were fun to engage in, especially when so many people were watching you.

Harper mouthed a final goodbye to Gwen, closed her eyes, and dissipated under Moxxi's touch. She left the room as a shimmering mist. Machines beeped and within a few moments, thirty-seven-year-old Harper opened her eyes.

Moxxi solidified their own appearance so Harper knew she wasn't alone.

"Thank you," She squeaked, her vocal cords rusty from lack of use.

"Of course," Moxxi insisted. "You gonna be okay?"

"Yeah. Take care of them." Harper paused in thought. "Will you come find me after?"

Moxxi hadn't been planning on that. "I don't know where I'll be by then. Do you know where you'll be after all this?"

Harper pursed her lips. "No. I guess not."

"I wish you nothing but the best, Harper. None of us would have survived without you."

She blushed. "And I guess you weren't totally useless after all." Her fingers poked out from underneath the blankets and gestured to the length of her body.

"Ha. I guess not. You take good care of yourself. Allow your family to love on you. You deserve that in your life."

"I'll miss all of you." Harper's words caught in her throat.

"We'll never be that far away." Moxxi squeezed her hand and faded out of sight.

When Moxxi returned to their shadow form, everyone else had left the room. They were congregated out in the hall.

"What's going on?"

Jade spoke for the tearful group. "We decided it'd be best if Gwen waited for you outside after this."

"Outside of Harper's room?" Moxxi looked for the tween and saw her kicking the corner of a wall off in the distance, avoiding the group as best as she could.

"Outside of the hospital would be the most ideal location." Jade's delivery was firm. "This is an overwhelming time for her, and she would be better suited out there instead of attending other hospital rooms."

She's speaking very firmly about someone she just met. Moxxi didn't mind, but they didn't imagine the kids would love that idea. "And everyone is cool with that?"

"Everyone is sympathetic to Gwen's heart-ache."

Moxxi was not so sure how true that was. They went over to discreetly check on Gwen. "Did you want to meet outside then?"

"That will be good. I will just wait here a little longer. I want to make sure that they see her awake first."

"Understood. I'll be out for you soon." Moxxi felt the urge to squeeze Gwen's shoulder, or hand, or anything to offer physical emotional support, but that was too strange and foreign to Moxxi. They were sure they'd have done it wrong if they tried. They were no Harper.

Jade approved of the interaction. “That’s settled. Shall we go back to our room?” Jade asked her children.

Jade was pushy, but Moxxi didn’t want to play leader so they were happy to have her take on that role.

The kids' energy had been drained. They did what was expected of them, but it was evident that their enormous hearts in their tiny bodies were making it hard on them. Upon entering the room, Azi gave his mother a huge hug and a kiss and sat next to his designated hospital bed. Amari could not be separated.

“Can we just get this done? This is so lame,” Azi requested, emotionally spent.

“I can. Is that what you want?” Moxxi approached the subject delicately.

“Yeah. I guess.” Azi held the hands of his doppelganger before him. “I love you, mom. See you soon, Amari.”

“All my love, my brave special boy.” Jade didn’t hide her tears this time.

Moxxi wanted this to go quickly for everyone. They placed their hands on the bodies of Azi. The room stayed quiet as they all watched Azi’s soul turn into a sparkling dust. Azi had been successfully transported back to his original form.

With Azi gone, half of Jade began to turn into a translucent green hue. She held her daughter closer and shuffled them both over to Amari’s bed. “How about we go together?" Jade maneuvered her daughter into place and held her hands over Amari's.

Amari's resistance was not discrete; she held onto her mother with all her might, but she didn't fight or cry.

Jade gave Moxxi the go ahead, but Moxxi wanted it from Amari, whose face was buried and not visible to the outside world.

Azi coughed in his bed. Machines beeped just like they had for Harper. "Amari?" He rolled to see his sister. "Amari, where are you?" His hand was shaking as he reached out to touch her.

"Go, be with your brother. He needs you. You'll always have me right here," Jade encouraged.

"Amari?" He was panicking. "Amari!"

Voices were startling outside.

"It's time," Jade announced.

"It's time," Amari repeated.

Moxxi's hands found their placement, and in one fell swoop, Amari and Jade turned to mist together.

"Here," Amari croaked, her voice raspy and shallow. "I'm here, Azi." She dangled her hand out the bed. They were still a few feet apart.

Moxxi bumped the two beds as doctors filled the room so the twins could touch. Moxxi supervised from the shadows long enough to know that everything was set health wise before walking into the chaos in their more tangible form.

A nurse blocked Moxxi's way almost instantly.

"Who are you? I don't see a visitor's badge on you. You're going to have to check in at the desk."

"I'm their sister." Moxxi lied.

"I haven't heard about no sister in the year these kids have been here. I don't believe you. You're going to need to go to that desk and show some ID to the lady in charge. We're busy here." The nurse was stepping forward to push Moxxi out.

"I was overseas, but I'm back. I just want to see my siblings."

The nurse talked low and steady. "I don't know who you are, but I know these kids have no other kin in this country, so whatever it is you're trying to do, let this family have peace and get. Otherwise, my finger is already on the button to call security, and I am happy to have you removed from the premises."

Ugh! I'm the one trying to help them! Not you! "I'll go sign in, get my badge, and I'll be right back."

"We'll just see about that, won't we?"

Moxxi yelled in their fullest voice. "Hang tight kids, I just have to go sign in."

The nurse raised the phone to page security while the twins sang out together, "Okay, Moxxi! We're not going anywhere."

There was no line at the visitor's station, but Moxxi had no idea how they could pull this off. "Hi, I need to check in please."

"Just fill out that sheet there with your name and who you're here to see."

Moxxi did as directed. Unsure of what their last

name would be they first wrote down Mors, but they felt it was a little too on the nose so added an extra "e" at the end.

The nurse clicked some keys on the keyboard. "Looks like those patients are only accepting family at this time. Are you family?"

"I am."

"Hmm. Okay. Then I just need to see some I.D."

Moxxi had never had a piece of identification in their life. "I don't have that."

"Then I'm sorry, but I can't let you in."

Moxxi was going to protest; they would change back into a shadow and transport the kids if they had to, but a wheelchair hit them in the shins first. "Ow!"

A familiar laugh chuckled below. It was Harper. "What's going on here?"

Moxxi didn't understand how they were out and about so quickly. "I was just telling this nice lady that I'm here to see my siblings."

"I'm so glad you're here!" Harper laid on thick. "Maxine, this is my sister's child I was telling you about! The fancy one! This is Moxxi . . ." Harper tried to read the sign in sheet as well as she had read the nurse's name tag. "I am so ashamed, but I forgot your married name. You're no longer a Coca anymore! Time sure does fly."

"Silly Aunt Harper. I'm a Morse now."

"I'd forget my head if it wasn't attached, I swear!" Harper winked. "Maxine, did you get that?

Moxxi Morse. It should all be right there."

Waves of facial expressions crossed the nurse's face. Defiance, confusion, anger, and then, finally, acceptance. "How exciting to have your family together again." She reached for a visitor's pass and wrote the room number down on it. "You two have a lovely day now, you hear!"

Moxxi smiled politely then pulled Harper into a corner before pressing on. "What was THAT? I mean thank you, but whoa!"

"A lady never reveals her secrets." They took Moxxi's hand and pressed something into it. "Now let's go see those babies. If I remember correctly, not all of their family is as honest and humble as we are."

Moxxi opened their hand to see a wooden mallet. A wooden mallet that used to be golden. "This was your gift from Daikokuten."

"And I used it, albeit accidentally, to give you all safe travels home."

This was exactly the win that the twins needed. Moxxi grabbed the back of Harper's wheelchair and took her to the kids' room. It was still packed with medical personnel, and the nurse spotted Moxxi's return before they even made it to the door.

"Security this is who I was telling you about!"

Moxxi mustered up some fake confidence. "Hello. I'm Moxxi Morse; this is my Aunt Harper. I may have broken a few rules earlier and come here without my visitor's pass, my apologies. It's all fixed now though." She held it out to the two people in uniform.

"And I'm in room 817, so no visitor's pass for me, but Maxine downstairs would be happy to vouch for me." Harper turned towards the defiant nurse. "In fact, Janice, I think we've even met a handful of times. Isn't that right?"

The nurse blocking the way was displeased in her response, but she couldn't stop it from coming. "That's right. We've met a few times."

Security gave the pass back to Moxxi and apologized for the confusion. Moxxi waited until they were out of sight to wipe the sweat from their brow.

Harper kept on chatting up the nurse, Janice. "I believe Moxxi here has the best set of instructions here on how to help those two sweet kiddos now that they've awoken. Can you be a doll and help Moxxi out with whatever they need? I heard her instructions came from Jade herself!"

Janice glared at Moxxi. "I'll help Moxxi with whatever they need."

Moxxi felt vaguely threatened by Janice's declaration of support.

Ignorant to the tone of the room, Harper cheered, "Love to hear it!"

As Harper celebrated her triumph, the mallet turned to dust in Moxxi's hand.

"Kids! Auntie and Sister are here!" She wheeled herself in, speaking faster than she ever had to anyone that would listen about her new fake life.

"Thank the Gods!" Moxxi whispered to themself and out of the corner of their eye, they saw a tiny mouse scamper along a tall bookcase after giving an approving nod.

Epilogue

"You're sure this is a good idea? I'm starting to seriously second guess myself here." Moxxi's stomach churned as they walked up to the elaborate mansion.

"Everyone second guesses themself when they're near Chromwell. That's natural. It's how you're supposed to feel," Lena assured.

"Bright Eyes, I don't know about this. Maybe I was wrong, and this is a horrible idea," Moxxi countered.

"Listen, as much as I have grown to adore Azariah and Amari, they can't live at my house forever. They also can't live with Selene forever, despite what he says. Master Chromwell is a good choice, plus Ina is the absolute sweetest."

"Yeah, but what about Averi? Don't they live with some type of monstrous beast that tried to eat you?"

"He has a padlock on his door. It's fine. There's

way less protection in Ward A for way worse out there." Arriving at the top of the steps, Lena prepped her friend. "Here we go. Ready?" She used the gilded knockers on the door. The entrance swung open slowly with a creek.

"What is this? A horror movie?"

"Stop it! She can hear you!" Lena thwapped Moxxi's chest. "Hello? Anyone here?"

"In here, darling!"

"That's Ina. She's the good one!" Lena pulled Moxxi along to the kitchen.

Aren't they both supposed to be good?

"Lena! Pleasure to see you! How's that latest addition to Ward A? I heard they're a doozie!"

Lena stuck out her tongue. "They're a hot mess, but you know who isn't? My friend here that I brought you to meet! This is Moxxi! Moxxi, this is Ina."

In all the things Lena Basil had said as she gushed over Ina, she forgot to mention the expansive angelic wingspan and her even superior beauty.

"A friend of Lena's is a friend of mine! It's nice to meet you!" Ina stuck out her hand to shake Moxxi's.

Moxxi was stunned but tried to act socially acceptable.

Ina waited for the new friend to speak but was happy to fill the gap in their stead. "What brings you to Astoria, Moxxi? Were you once a pupil at Legacy Academy?"

Another voice chimed from around the corner. "If they were, I don't know how they'd have met

Lena." Master Chromwell entered the room, covered in soot and scorch marks.

That does not make me feel better about my choices.

Lena ignored the snide remark and kept her focus with Ina. "Moxxi was actually the one who helped Dhruva with the Nulls. They're a transporter. They work under Mors. Have you ever met Mors?"

"Hmm. No. I don't believe I have, but my roster of gods is much less impressive than Theodora's." Ina smiled as her counterpart placed a kiss on her cheek.

"Ina is too kind. But no. I haven't spent much time with the Roman gods. I do not have the best track record with that pantheon so it was best to quit before things got even worse."

That must be a reference to Invidia. Moxxi had heard all about what happened with Mrs. Basil while they were gone. They were glad she was happy and healthy now, but what a disaster it was to get there. "You are probably not missing out," Moxxi joked.

Everyone laughed. *Everyone understood my joke and laughed.* That had never happened. *Maybe this isn't so bad after all.* A warm feeling began to brew in Moxxi's chest.

"Forgive me if I'm being too forward, child." Master Chromwell began. "But, you see, I have this little staff that I use time and time again, and well, when I use it, I can see things others can't. And I haven't let Ina on to any of these dealings, but if my talents serve me properly, I believe you are in need of our assistance. Do I have that right?"

Ina sighed. "Theodora, you can't go around telling people their business. We've talked about that. Let them choose what they disclose to you."

"Yes, yes. You're probably right, but in this particular instance, I'm very interested."

That was a red flag to Moxxi. "You are? Why?"

"I, uh—well, I—" Master Chromwell kept glancing from Ina to Moxxi. "Now you know we're a little older, Ina and I, and well, we missed our window for certain life events because of, well, other life events." She intertwined her fingers with the angel's. "And while some of those things are fine to miss out on, there are others that are a bit more challenging to let go of. Emotionally, that is."

Lena clasped her mouth. "Ohmygosh! You want kids!!!"

Everyone stared at Lena with wide eyes.

"Is that where this is all going?" Ina asked, jovially. "Do you need a family, Moxxi?"

Their entire body screamed yes, but they refused to let themself speak.

"No! Not Moxxi! There are two twins. They are very cute, very energetic, very . . ." Lena wanted to choose the right word. ". . . special." She let that sink in. "The kind of special you are masterful with, Ms. Chromwell."

"Me? I've never raised a child. Ina is the motherly one, next to your own, of course."

"You watched over Selene . . . and Kohl." Lena

treaded carefully with that last name. “As well as hundreds of other kids at Legacy. These twins have poorly contained raw talent. They need someone who will keep them safe.”

Moxxi found words they were able to speak. “Lena’s right. Safety is a prime concern for them. There are people looking for them.”

“Oh no.” Ina gasped. “People know what these children can do?”

Moxxi was heartfelt in their response. “They do. It was their mother’s dying wish that I did my best to help them find someone that could protect them in her absence. Legacy Academy was my best bet. Lena led me here.”

“Their mother has passed, you said. What about their father?” Master Chromwell was deep into thought.

Moxxi stumbled over their words.

Ina stepped in. “He’s why you're here.”

Moxxi was relieved by the angel’s understanding. *Lena was right about her.* They nodded. “That’s true, ma’am.”

Master Chromwell cracked a smile. “Do you know these children?”

“Recently so, but yes. We’ve spent a significant amount of time together.”

“What do you think of them?”

That I love them and I shouldn’t have to beg someone to take them in when they’re such a gift to the world. That if my life was different, I’d have claimed them myself and never even come here. "They are the best five-year-olds I know. Almost to be six, actually. They are wily, but their heart is beyond anything I've ever encountered in my time here on Earth."

Ina leaned towards her partner. "I believe them when they say that. They have a full heart."

"Yes, it seems they are true to their word." Theodora agreed, but wanted to dig deeper into the situation presenting itself. "If we open our doors to them, would you choose to drop in and check on the twins, or is your intention to consider your obligation fulfilled once they have been handed off to a suitable sponsor?"

I don't want them to have a sponsor. I want them to have a family. They deserve a mother, their mother. Moxxi didn't want to blow it for the kids, though. Theodora hadn't said yes, but she hadn't said no either. "I suppose that would be up to you and Ina, should you choose to welcome them into your home and treat them as your own." They worried they emphasized the last part of that sentence a little too strongly.

Lena could tell this wasn't going as smoothly as she anticipated. "It could be nice, you know? My mom is with them now. She and Selene are obsessed with the tiny tykes."

That caught Chromwell off guard. "Millie has met the children?"

Moxxi affirmed Lena's statement. "She's

watching them right now and has been most of the week."

"Millie is very good at raising children," Ina asserted. "Would Millie be a—"

Lena cut her mentor off. "No!"

"I see." Ina giggled.

Moxxi gave Lena an unpleasant stare.

"It's nothing against the kids, but we have the three of us, my boyfriend, a raptor dragon thing with a best friend who happens to be a very cheeky golem, and sometimes a Sumerian goddess and a lion griffin. Casa Basil is at full occupancy."

Ina was covering her face, hiding her amusement.

"With that information brought forth, it does seem that Millie is adamantly unavailable at this point of time." Theodora posed to her better half.

Ina grinned. "I think you're a swell second choice, my dear. Some may even say you're their top pick."

"It's sooner than we expected," Theodora cautioned.

Ina waived her hand nonchalantly. "It was always going to happen when the gods deemed it so. I find I seldom have control over my life's biggest events. All except this one." Ina pulled her partner's hand to her chest.

"It has been predestined," Master Chromwell declared. "Moxxi, we would be honored to take in your little ones and protect them and love them and care for them for the rest of our days."

Relief and sadness spread through Moxxi. "Thank you. Shall I bring them by tomorrow?"

"Tomorrow? Are they not in our neighbor's house?" Ina asked.

Theodora steadied Ina's words. "Tomorrow will be a fine day to come by. That will give everyone the time they need."

Ina caught on to the hidden message she had previously missed. "Oh, yes. Yes, I can see that. Tomorrow will be splendid. Can you please tell us some of their favorite foods? I would like to have the house full of goodies for them!" Ina reached out for Moxxi. "Here, can I show you what we have? It's a rather vast selection!"

They took the angel's hand and held it through the tour of the kitchen.

Lena drew near her former Headmistress. "You had me worried for a second there."

"And why is that, Miss Basil?"

"You were grilling Moxxi pretty hard. I was worried you were going to say no."

"One needs to know the things one needs to know."

"I thought cultivating two powerful kiddos would be a shoe in with you."

"I couldn't agree more."

"Then why the pointed questions?" Lena was getting annoyed at Master Chromwell's indirectness.

"Because, dear Basil, what you lack to see, per

usual, is the question that actually needs to be asked."

"If you're both able to take in the two wild children under your wings?"

Chromwell sighed while meeting Lena's squinty face. "No, Magdalena, not if we'll take in two. I was trying to parse out if we were actually being asked to take in three."

"Why would Moxxi need to be taken in? They've been on their own their whole life. They're the poster child for independence."

"Precisely, dear Basil. Precisely." Theodora watched as Ina stood, hand in hand, with Moxxi as they pointed to various items in the open cabinets. She watched as Moxxi leaned their head near Ina's shoulder without actually touching it, and how Ina tested the waters in reciprocating the same action until the pair was standing in the open space, leaning on each other, feeling safe, feeling secure, and forming the roots of what having a family could mean to each of them.

Acknowledgments

I am a broken record when it comes to these, but as always I am forever grateful for my anchors in the storm of life: Z, B, and Dj.

Z - Writing this with you was one of the greatest joys of my life. We had no idea that one that car ride home, where you were so sick, and I asked you to help me come up with character name ideas to distract you that it would lead to this. You picked the perfect name all those years ago and you have only increased your talent since then. Thank you for sharing your ideas and opinions with me from the good to the bad. Everything you say has value and I hope you feel seen and admired in our first novella together.

B - You went from having to deal with one writer in the house to two. While our ups are high, the downs are low. Thank you for your never-ending patience and guidance while both of us navigated this passion project. It's never a dull moment, but it feels safer to fly knowing you're ready to catch both of us if something knocks us down.

Dj - I am not quite sure who would sing your praises louder out of Z and I. You carry the team on your back. From being there during conception, to the first words on the page, being one of the first readers, editing, cover design, formatting, uploading. You're our right-hand man through and through. Thank you for helping every time you can and standing by us when we have to navigate things outside of our control. Z and I can often come in like opposing hurricanes and I'm eternally grateful that you weather our storms.

Additionally, in this go round, I would also like to give a special shoutout to another author who goes above and beyond in her friendship and in her critiques: Courtney Ellis. You took a story with good bones and helped shape it into a beautiful Roman sculpture. Your time and attention to detail were invaluable. Thank you for being a friend.

About the Author

A. P. Goodman is a lifelong enthusiast of mythology and religion. From her first love of Disney's Hercules to her most recent love of Japanese mythos, Ashley has spent much of her time engrossed in various accounts of past and present lore. She loves obscure stories best and feels strongly that no tale should be left untold. In her moments outside of cultural deep dives, she feels nothing compares to warm chai and creating core memories. Her loved ones and pets (especially her fluffy puppy) are always her favorite company. She also has two meddlesome cats and a bunny who reigns as king of the household. *Pursuits of Moxxi - The Backrooms* is the first in their new novella series and was written in collaboration with their kiddo.

www.ingramcontent.com/pod-product-compliance
Lightning Source LLC
Chambersburg PA
CBHW061242170626
46809CB00007B/2792

* 9 7 8 1 9 6 4 9 8 0 0 2 7 *